Crush

Crush

Stories by
Ellen Conford

HarperCollins*Publishers*

For my Scrabble group:
Mary Capalbi, Bob Frey, Dee Jackson,
and Marjorie Schoneboom—dear friends,
through good tiles and bad

Library of Congress Cataloging-in-Publication Data
Conford, Ellen.
    Crush / stories by Ellen Conford.
        p.   cm.
    Summary: A series of nine romantic episodes in the lives of B.J. and other
students at Cutter's Forge High as they plan for the Valentine's Day Sweetheart Stomp.
    ISBN 0-06-025414-9. — ISBN 0-06-025415-7 (lib. bdg.)
    [1. Dating (Social customs)—Fiction. 2. Interpersonal relations—Fiction. 3. High
Schools—Fiction. 4. Schools—Fiction.] I. Title.
PZ7.C7593Cr   1998   97-34335
[Fic]—dc21   CIP
                                                                                          AC

Typography by Steve Scott
1   2   3   4   5   6   7   8   9   10
❖
First Edition

24396

SC
FIC
CON

10/12/00

#14.95

Contents

Room
202

"Tickets for the Sweetheart Stomp are still available at the student government office, Room 114, during lunch hours or half an hour before and after school. Celebrate Valentine's Day in our elegant gym. Fumigated specially for the occasion. Dance the night away to the romantic strains of Yellow Fever, everyone's favorite really loud band.

"Enjoy the lavish buffet of bologna roll-ups, Kool-Aid, and gourmet potato chips—the kind with *ridges*. Tickets are only seven dollars apiece, or the special bargain price of fourteen dollars a pair."

B.J. Green only half listened to the announcement. She didn't expect to go to the dance. No one had asked her, and she certainly wasn't bold enough to ask someone herself. The closest contact she'd had with a boy was when she'd bumped—literally—into Doug Meyers at the mall just before Christmas.

A girl with more social skills or a quicker wit might have used the collision to strike up a conversation. But Doug had seemed more concerned with retrieving his spilled packages than with getting to know B.J.

She thought, not for the first time, what a dumb name Sweetheart Stomp was for a Valentine's Day dance. Not that she wouldn't want to go to it, but it sounded like an event where you stomped your sweetheart unconscious.

But the social bigwigs at Cutter's Forge High were heavy into alliteration this year. They'd called the Halloween dance the Halloween Hoedown, even though there was no country music and it wasn't a square dance. The Thanksgiving dance was the Turkey Trot, which almost made sense, since B.J. knew that back in the 1920s or so the turkey trot had actually been a dance step.

For Christmas they'd had the Holiday Hop. And now the dance committee had come up with the Sweetheart Stomp.

B.J. sighed and looked around at her classmates. Mr. Tortola's homeroom was buzzing with the excited whispers of predance planning. The event was eight days away. B.J. was sure that everyone else had already found their dates, bought their outfits, arranged their evening.

There would be get-togethers before the dance and parties afterward, which would prolong the Valentine's Day festivities into the early hours of February 15th.

B.J. wouldn't be attending any of them.

She looked across the aisle at Amy Porter. Amy was drawing hearts on the back cover of her notebook: "AP + HB" The B stood for Batso, Amy's boyfriend. His real name was Henry Batkowski.

Amy and Henry probably wouldn't be going to any of the parties either. But Amy wouldn't care. She never seemed to worry about whether people liked her or not.

The PA announcements droned on. B.J. looked across two rows at Linda Sherman. She'd be going with Will Moffet. B.J. wouldn't trust the girl to baby-sit a pet ferret, but Will was so smitten with her that he dropped forty IQ points whenever she was around.

Di Callahan was examining her eyelashes in a tiny eye-shadow compact. Her only problem would be deciding which boy to go with. She'd probably have to choose among seventeen ardent candidates. Her Royal Blondness used up boys like Kleenex.

Jamie Farrentino, chin in her hand, was gazing dreamily at Alexei Grigorov. Alexei was a Russian exchange student who was staying with Teddy Klein for the semester. Alexei was a mystery wrapped in an enigma. He didn't say much, but he smiled a lot. And he was very conscientious. His head was always buried in a book, he took notes compulsively, and his eyes were intent on whoever was speaking to him, as if he were trying to lip-read English. Slim, dark, handsome . . . *Forget about it!* B.J. ordered herself. If she couldn't talk to a boy in English, how in the world would she communicate with one in Russian?

Robert La Motte. *Not.* Not going to the dance, not going to be anyone's Valentine, even more out of the dating loop than B.J. He'd always been a nerd. He'd never called himself anything but Robert. Not Bob, Bobby, or Rob. Always Robert. And he wasn't even a smart nerd. When called on in class, he turned red and mumbled, or just shook his head and stared down at his desk.

You wouldn't expect a boy like Robert to be well-dressed—not that decent clothes would make much difference. His build was slim to none, and he had trouble walking and talking at the same time. Actually, he had trouble talking at all.

He won't be stomping his sweetheart, B.J. thought. And then felt immediately guilty for making fun of him—even if only to herself.

Laurel Baker. She was going to the dance with

Teddy. They were just friends, but B.J. had seen them buying their tickets two days ago.

The bell rang. "Okay, settle down," Mr. Tortola said. He pulled out his roll book.

"Cloris Ackerman?"

"Here."

"Laurel Baker?"

"Here."

"Kate Axelrod?"

"Here."

"Henry Batkowski?"

"Yo."

Amy Porter grinned. B.J. watched enviously as Amy drew two more entwined hearts on her notebook.

The Gifts of the Mangy

*V*alentine's Day was only a day away, and Amy Porter still hadn't found a gift for Batso.

Of course, his real name wasn't Batso. It was Henry Batkowski, but everyone called him Batso. Most people thought he was a little batty anyway. Most people thought Amy was a little batty too. But Amy didn't care about anyone else's opinion. She thought Batso was adorable.

In private she called him Bugbear. He pretended to be annoyed by this nickname, and threatened to punch her lights out if she ever used it in public. But Amy knew perfectly well he would never punch anyone's lights out, let alone hers. Despite his looks, Batso was gentle as a lamb.

Valentine's Day would be their six-month anniversary, a fact that struck Amy as extremely romantic.

She wanted to do something really special to mark

the event. They'd be going to the Sweetheart Stomp, even though Bugbear was not the school-dance type.

He was not comfortable on the dance floor. In fact, he wasn't that comfortable anywhere in school. He felt most at ease on his motorcycle or working under the hood of the ancient, rusting Jaguar he was fixing up.

Batso didn't just love Amy. He admired her. She was the smartest girl he knew, which was why he kept trying to teach her how to take care of her own car. He knew she could learn to change her oil, replace her plugs, and check her tire pressure in a mere matter of hours. It drove him nuts that she didn't even know how to work a self-serve gas pump—and had no intention of learning.

"Don't you realize how much money you could save?" Batso would plead. "Okay, forget rotating your tires—that's heavy lifting. But if you'd just use the self-serve gas, you'd save four cents a gallon."

"That's only forty-eight cents on a fill-up," Amy argued. She held out her hands. "And what if something happened to *these*?" She fluttered her fingers. "Do you know how much a manicure costs?"

Batso didn't know, but he figured it was plenty. Especially for the kind Amy got. Her nails were, in his opinion, dangerously long and absurdly decorated.

Every two weeks she'd emerge from Sofronia's Nail Salon with her inch-long fingernails embellished with some new kind of nonsense. One week it would be tiny silver stars and crescent moons stenciled into midnight-blue polish. Blue nail polish, for Pete's sake! Next time it might be fake jewel chips stuck onto slick blood-red lacquer.

Once she had even had her nails painted black with a thin white strip down the center of each, except for her index fingers, which were done in alternating black and white stripes. Batso thought stripes belonged on zebras.

Amy's nails were her pride and joy. And they were the only thing—or, to be more precise—the only ten things that Batso didn't like about her.

Batso couldn't figure it out. Amy was not the kind of girl who fussed much about how she looked. She didn't dress to impress. She mostly wore baggy khakis, tight jeans, and T-shirts with odd messages, like UKRAINIAN BEET FESTIVAL and SAVE THE NARWHALS.

She bought a lot of her clothes at the Army-Navy store. Sometimes she even picked up some old stuff at the First Baptist Bargain Box, a church thrift shop.

She never wore makeup, as far as Batso could tell. Anyway, nothing on her face ever rubbed off on his face, and he loved her clean, natural look. No cosmetic, he thought, could make her cuter than she already was.

So this obsession with her nails—the hours and money she spent every two weeks at Sofronia's, the resistance to any hands-on automotive experience—was a mystery to him.

Besides, they were dangerous. Simply holding hands was a challenge. Her nails almost always scraped his knuckles or the backs of his wrists. When she put her arms around him, they dug into his neck.

Last October, she'd played touch football with Batso and his brothers. Trying to intercept a pass, she had actually jabbed him in the eye and scratched his cornea. For two weeks he had looked like he was crying. Amy had been guilt-stricken. But she didn't cut her nails. She just swore off football.

Amy knew that Batso didn't like her nails.

He'd tried to be subtle about it. "Did you see on the news last night," he asked her once, "about the dangers of fingernail fungus?"

Another time he clipped an article from the *National Enquirer* about the risk of infection from unsanitary conditions in nail salons. He even showed her the cut on his scalp where one of her little jewels had nicked him when she'd gotten her nails hopelessly tangled in his hair.

But Amy didn't trim her nails. She just stopped trying to run her hands through his hair.

The truth was, Batso's hair was the only thing Amy didn't like about *him*. Not that it wasn't great hair. It was gorgeous hair. Amy told him that all the time. It was thick and dark, and Batso kept it very clean, shampooing at least once a day. But it was so long, it hung down past his shoulder blades. It took forever to dry, and he didn't style it at all. Sometimes he twisted a rubber band around it and made a ponytail. But Batso had a high forehead, and when he pulled his hair back, he looked like he had a receding hairline.

When she rode behind him on his motorcycle, Amy frequently found herself being slapped in the face by flying hair, which was dangerous because it would get in her eyes and her mouth, so she had to hold on to Batso with one hand and brush hair from her eyes and mouth with the other.

"You know, Bugbear," she'd tell him, "you'd look great in a style like this." And she'd show him a magazine picture of a man with wavy hair that swooped down over the forehead and curved gracefully behind the ears.

But Batso didn't think so. "I'd look like a wuss," he'd say.

Because his hair took so long to dry, Batso ran around in all kinds of weather with it wet. Amy worried about him getting the flu, or pneumonia—at the very least, an ear infection—by having his wet head constantly exposed to the winter's frigid winds. "It can't be good for you to be out in the freezing cold with your hair soaking wet," she'd tell him.

"Germs make you sick," Batso would say. "Wet hair has nothing to do with it."

Amy thought she understood why Batso didn't want to cut his hair. He'd been growing it for years— just as she'd been growing her nails, ever since she'd stopped biting them—and he was used to the way he looked. She knew how scary it was to cut long hair short. Lots of girls agonized over it for months, and almost needed anesthesia when they finally told the hairdresser, "Go on, *do* it!"

And she knew that Batso couldn't completely understand why she was so vain about her nails, even though she'd explained to him how they were her own personal red (or black-and-white) badges of courage.

Amy had bitten her nails for years. She'd tried— and failed—everything in an effort to stop. Every January 1st she resolved to break the habit, and every January 5th she was gnawing at them again.

She tried keeping her hands in her pockets, sitting on them, snapping rubber bands against her wrists every time she started to bite. Nothing worked. She coated her nails with a mixture of Vaseline, chili powder, and Tabasco sauce, so they'd taste awful. But that didn't stop her either. She just developed an intense craving for Mexican food.

She simply couldn't control the habit. It was like any other addiction that overpowered its victims. She didn't know why she did it—she just knew she couldn't stop. She'd wondered if there was a twelve-step program for confirmed nail-biters. There wasn't.

And then, a year ago last April, she'd had a brainstorm. She and her mother were clearing out the hall closet when Amy found an old pair of yellow leather driving gloves.

The gloves had tapered fingers, circular cutouts over the knuckles, and little straps that clipped at the wrists.

"Good grief," Amy's mother said. "It *has* been a long time since we went through this stuff. Those gloves must have been there for twenty years."

Amy pulled them on and held out her hands to examine the effect.

"Cool," she said. "Very retro."

"Well, take them if you want them," Mrs. Porter said. "But let's store them with the winter things. You won't need them till next year."

"No," Amy said. She sat down on the bottom step of the staircase. *"No."* She looked up at her mother, looked down at the gloves. Her eyes shone.

"You know what I just realized? I never bite my nails when I've got gloves on. So all I have to do is leave the gloves on."

"All the time?" her mother asked.

"All the time," Amy said.

And she did. Right through April and May and half of June. She wore the gloves at home, at school, in bed.

The first week she often found herself trying to chew right through the leather to get at a fingernail, but she resisted the impulse to yank the glove off.

Using a computer keyboard was a challenge. On the plus side, her gym teacher was astounded by her improvement in rope climbing.

Of course, people were curious about why she was wearing gloves everywhere, all the time, in April and May. She just explained, with her usual frankness, that she was trying to stop biting her nails.

"What a great idea!" a couple of girls said. A few

days later they were wearing gloves too. All the time. Everywhere.

By the end of May, Amy's nails were so long that the gloves didn't fit anymore.

Her mother presented Amy with a gift certificate to Sofronia's Nail Salon. "I'm so impressed with you," she said. "It's hard to kick a habit like that, but you did it."

Amy went for her first manicure, and never bit her nails again.

Was it any wonder that she was proud of her accomplishment? Was it any wonder that she didn't want to cut her nails short? They represented a triumph of willpower, a victory of self-control.

It was even harder for her to use a computer now than it had been when she had gloves on, but Amy didn't care. Every time she looked at her long, strong nails, she told herself, "If I can do this, I can do *anything*."

Except, of course, convince Batso to cut his hair.

Now, only twenty-four hours before Valentine's Day and their six-month anniversary, Amy drummed her fingers (carefully) on her desk, staring at the piece of paper in front of her. POSSIBLE ANNIVERSARY/VALENTINE GIFTS FOR BUGBEAR was printed at the top. The rest of the paper was absolutely blank.

Her eyes wandered, as they often did, to her fingers. She'd gotten a truly outstanding manicure for the dance. The polish was a pearly pink, and in the center of each nail was a sweet little red heart. On one thumb was stenciled a delicate *B*; on the other, an *A*.

To commemorate their Valentine's Day anniversary. Bugbear would love it.

Suddenly Amy threw down her pen. *No, he won't,* she told herself. *He doesn't like long nails. He's never liked long nails. Putting a* B *on one of them isn't going to prove I love him.*

And then it hit her. The perfect gift; probably the only gift Batso wanted from her.

She looked at her hands again—at the long, tapering nails, at the festive, fanciful decorations. *No,* she thought. *No! Why should I? After I worked so hard to grow them? After so many years of trying? Why should I cut my nails for Batso when he won't cut his hair for me?*

Because I love him, the answer came. *And because he's more important than manicures. And because I don't bite them anymore, and I know I'm strong and I don't need long nails to remind me that I can accomplish anything I want.*

She headed for the bathroom. She got her father's nail clippers from the medicine cabinet. She collected a wad of cotton balls and a bottle of nail polish remover from her mother's vanity.

She held the clippers next to her left thumb and took a deep breath. She wanted to close her eyes so she wouldn't have to witness the massacre. But of course she couldn't do that, not without risking injury.

Click! Off came the thumbnail. She gulped and told herself she'd be able to play football again. *Click!* Off came the index nail. *I won't keep hitting the wrong keys on the computer*, she thought. *Click!* The middle fingernail. *Think of what I can buy with all the money I'll save on manicures.*

When she was finished cutting and wiping off the polish, she looked down at her bare, pale, stubby nails and nearly burst into tears.

She didn't know whether she felt noble and selfless, or just stupid and submissive.

Batso wouldn't do this for me, she told herself again. *He wouldn't hack off his hair to prove he loved me.*

But he doesn't have to, she realized. *I know he loves me. Even when I scratch his cornea and gouge his scalp.* And as she put away the clippers and the nail polish remover, she had another inspiration.

She ran down the stairs, grabbed her jacket from the hall closet, and headed out for Shop 'n' Save.

Amy had actually bought a new dress for the Sweetheart Stomp. Well, it wasn't exactly new. She'd found it in the back room of the First Baptist Bargain Box. But it was certainly a startling change from what she usually wore.

It was red silk with spaghetti straps, a matching belt, and a narrow skirt that flared out in a kicky ruffle just above her knees. It looked like something Marilyn Monroe might have worn in an old movie.

Long, beautiful nails would have been dazzling with it. Instead Amy wore a pair of elbow-length red satin gloves she'd found right near the dress rack. She thought she looked pretty dazzling anyway.

The doorbell rang at eight o'clock. She grabbed Bugbear's carefully wrapped gift—the one she had bought at Shop 'n' Save—and ran downstairs.

Her father was just ushering Batso inside. "Don't you look spiffy tonight!"

Amy stopped at the bottom step and stared. Batso was wearing a *suit*. A dark-blue, double-breasted suit. With a lime-green T-shirt. Of course, he had his leather bomber jacket over it and his helmet on, but he certainly did look spiffier than Amy had ever seen him.

He was holding a narrow, gift-wrapped box. He stared back at Amy.

"Wow," he breathed.

"Happy six-month anniversary," Amy said, and gave Bugbear her present.

"Ditto." He gulped and shoved his gift at her. "Happy Valentine's Day, too."

"Thank you." Amy pulled the bow off the top of the box and started picking the Scotch-taped ends.

"Wouldn't it be easier with your gloves off?" Batso suggested.

She felt only a twinge as she said, "Believe me, I can do anything with gloves on. I can't wait to see what it is."

"I think you'll really like it," Batso said. "When I saw it, I right away knew it was perfect for you."

"Open yours," Amy said, peeling off the tape.

"Oh, right." Batso shrugged out of his jacket and dropped it onto the banister. He pulled his motorcycle helmet off.

And Amy screamed.

"Your hair!" she wailed. "Your beautiful hair! What did you *do* to it?"

"I cut it," Batso said. "Like you wanted me to."

Batso hadn't just cut his hair. He'd shaved it off. All of it—except for a quarter of an inch of stubble.

"I didn't mean—" Amy stopped herself in the middle of the sentence. He'd *done* it. He'd cut his hair for her. True, his head resembled a fuzzy bowling ball. But imagine how much he must love her to let himself look like that!

"Oh, Bugbear." She sighed and tried not to cry.

Batso scowled and glanced at Amy's father to check his reaction to the nickname. But Mr. Porter was still reacting to Batso's haircut. He gawked, fascinated, like a rubbernecker at a car wreck.

"It'll grow back," Batso said, trying to figure out why she looked so upset. "And now you won't have to worry about me going around with wet hair and getting sick."

Amy started to laugh.

"What?" Batso asked. *"What?"*

"Open yours." She watched as he tore the paper off, lifted the lid of the box, and pulled out what was inside.

"Twelve hundred watts." Amy giggled. "Hot and cool settings. Special brush attachment. 'Uniquely designed for long hair.' "

For a moment Batso was speechless. "It's just," he

said finally, "what I needed. And my hair grows real fast. In a couple of months, I'll be using this every day. It's a perfect present."

Amy tore off the last bit of gift wrap on Batso's present to her. It was a sleek, cream-colored leather case with a little gold clip.

"It's lovely," she said, turning it over in her hands.

"Open it up," Batso said.

She tugged at the clip, and the case opened out like a book. Inside, neatly arranged behind elastic bands, were cuticle nippers, a nail buffer, manicure scissors, orange sticks, and four travel-size bottles of nail polish.

Amy started to laugh. She laughed so hard, she had to lean against the banister to try to catch her breath.

"What's so funny?" Batso demanded. "It's a manicure kit. It's got everything you need for a professional—"

Gasping, Amy pulled off one long, red glove. She held out her hand.

"Your nails!" Batso cried. "What happened to your nails? Is the other hand like that too?"

She nodded, and burst into a fresh fit of giggles.

"I didn't mean for you to—" He stopped himself.

What an incredible thing she had done! She had given up what she was proudest of. Just for him. Had anyone, except his mother, ever loved him so much?

"They'll grow back," Amy said, when she managed to catch her breath. "And I'll use this"—she stroked the leather case—"to keep them nice and short."

"Keep them any way you want!" Batso said.

They glanced at Amy's father. He cleared his throat. "I guess this is my cue to leave. Have fun at the dance."

When he was gone, Batso squatted down at the bottom of the staircase next to Amy. He took her hands in his. He looked into her eyes, picked up her ungloved hand, and kissed each stubby, bare little fingertip in turn.

"You," he whispered, "are the best present I ever got."

She rubbed her cheek against the soft stubble that used to be his hair.

"Oh, Bugbear," she sighed. "Ditto."

Have a Heart

*I*t's hard to admit that the girl you love is a scheming, underhanded con artist and even harder to justify still loving her after you've admitted it.

Even Linda's parents must have known about her scams, and they couldn't help loving her either— though certainly not in the same way I did.

Linda said they'd moved to Cutter's Forge because her parents didn't like the kids she was hanging around with. But I figure the family got away from their last residence one step before the sheriff.

Thinking about it now, I'm sure it's more likely that the parents of the kids she was hanging around with pressured the Shermans to leave town before Linda conned them out of their college funds.

Whatever. The fact is that the first time I laid eyes on Linda, I was hopelessly smitten.

I spotted her the minute she walked into homeroom. Her glossy black hair fell to her shoulders in a tumble of curls. Her skin was like white silk, with a faint pink glow high on her cheeks. Her eyes were dark blue, almost violet, so striking that I could see their color twenty feet away.

The carbon dioxide level must have gone up fifty percent as every guy in the room exhaled at once. I'm not sure I breathed. I was busy praying. *Let her take the seat next to me. Please, let her take the seat next to me.*

Incredibly, she did.

I volunteered to be her personal Welcome Wagon, and spent the next two weeks showing her around Cutter's Forge, introducing her to my friends (mostly the female ones) and guiding her through the halls to her classes.

By the end of those two weeks I worshiped the ground she walked on. And she let me.

She also let me kiss her. Her lips were like honey. And she melted in my arms—or maybe I was the one who melted; I'm not sure. But she murmured, "Oh, Will . . ." and I don't remember anything after that. Except for later, when I got home and challenged my brother, Matt, to a game of one-on-one in the driveway, and fouled him every time he tried to shoot a basket.

Linda was so different from most of the girls I had grown up with in Cutter's Forge. She was so . . .

well . . . *feminine*. Soft, sweet, cuddly, noncompetitive. She liked me to take care of her, give her advice. She made me feel—this sounds so stupid—*manly*.

One day, while I was explaining mutual funds (we had just studied them in an econ unit on the stock market), she got a faraway look in her eyes and touched a finger to her adorable bottom lip.

"This is so *fascinating*, Will," she murmured. "What you're saying is that the small investor is *empowered* by a mutual fund, so that he has the same opportunity as the big shot to buy into major corporations."

"Well, yeah," I said, startled by her quick grasp of the concept. "That's a good way to put it."

"Hmm."

Two days later Linda showed me a beautifully printed flyer for the "Clean, Green Investment Club: Environmentally sound companies for the small investor with a conscience."

"You made it sound so interesting," she said, "that I started reading about the stock market. Have you ever heard of investment clubs?"

"Uh, well, no," I admitted. "We just started studying this stuff Monday."

"I saw this TV show," she said, "about some women in South Carolina. They started an investment club. They pool their money to buy stocks. They've made a *fortune* in the market."

"Really?"

"Yes," she said. Her (incredibly long) eyelashes fluttered with excitement. "And I was thinking—of course, I don't know very much about it, not like you do—but if we got every kid in school to invest a mere ten dollars . . ."

Linda didn't get every kid in school to invest a mere ten dollars in the Clean, Green Investment Club. But she did convince sixty-three of them to join.

"I don't think we're going to make a fortune with only six hundred and thirty dollars to invest," I said.

"A lot of these companies are very small," Linda reassured me. "Their stocks don't cost much, so we can get a lot of diversification for our money."

"Diversification?" I repeated. "Boy, you are a fast learner."

"Oh, pooh." She lowered her eyes shyly. "I am not. You're just such a gifted teacher."

Linda said her father would use his connections to help us invest the money with brokers who would charge only a fraction of their usual fees. "That way, our profits won't be eaten up by commissions," she explained.

She polled all the members of the Clean, Green

Club to find out which of the stocks on her list they preferred. She'd filled two pages with the names of environmentally sound companies and descriptions of what they did, profits and losses they'd made in the last five years, and projections for future earnings.

"Where did you get this stuff?" I asked when she showed me the list.

"You can do anything with a computer," she said.

"I didn't know you had a computer."

"I don't really," she said. "It's my parents'; I can hardly turn it on without my father's help."

As it turned out, you can't make a fortune in the stock market with six hundred and thirty dollars. Three months later, Linda handed out dividend checks to all sixty-three members of the Clean, Green Club.

The members were not impressed with their profits.

"Ninety-five cents?" I said, staring at the check she'd handed me. "That's all we made in three months?"

"I know it doesn't seem like much," Linda said. "But Will, it's a nine-and-a-half-percent return on your money. Where else are you going to get a nine-and-a-half-percent return?"

"You're right about that," I agreed. "I guess it takes money to make money. We just didn't have enough capital to start with."

I helped her explain to the other disgruntled club

members how terrific it was to get nine-and-a-half-percent interest on their ten dollars when their bank savings accounts were only paying three and a half percent.

But I guess they didn't understand finance as well as Linda and I did.

"What am I going to do with a lousy ninety-five cents?" Mark Chetwin demanded.

"Reinvest it," Linda suggested. "If everyone reinvests their ninety-five cents, plus another ten dollars . . ."

But no one did. So that was the end of the Clean, Green Club.

By this time we'd finished our unit on the stock market, and I sort of lost interest in the whole investment thing, though not in Linda. So I never thought to ask exactly where the club's six hundred and thirty dollars' worth of stock was.

Linda came to our house for Thanksgiving dinner. Her parents had gone to Acapulco for the holiday weekend. I couldn't believe she chose to spend the day with me instead of lolling on the beach in Mexico.

She'd barely been introduced to my family when she pulled a bunch of little tickets from her bag. Printed on them was:

ST. ROSE OF SHARON CHRISTMAS RAFFLE—TO BENEFIT THE SCHOOL. WIN A CLASSIC 1959 CORVETTE! A GIANT-

SCREEN TV! A CAMCORDER! A NEW YORK CITY THEATER
WEEKEND! PLUS OTHER VALUABLE PRIZES.

"What's St. Rose of Sharon?" I asked.

"It's the school I used to go to," Linda said. "Will, wouldn't it be *fabulous* if you won the Corvette?"

"I didn't know you were Catholic," I said.

She looked up at me, her (gorgeous violet) eyes wide. "Is that a problem?"

"No, no!" I said. "I just didn't know you were religious. How many tickets can I buy?"

I bought a book of ten tickets, my aunt Sunny bought five tickets, my parents bought three tickets, my brother, Matt, bought two tickets. Even my bratty cousin Andrew, who is eight, bought a ticket.

"I love your family," Linda said, as we snuggled in the den after dinner.

"They loved you too," I said.

"Oh, Will, do you think so?" she asked. "I wanted them to like me. I hope they didn't think I was being too pushy selling the raffle tickets. But I thought, it's for *charity*. And if your family was as sweet as you . . ."

"How could anyone think you were pushy?" I asked, stroking the shoulder of her soft angora sweater.

She sold the raffle tickets at school, too. Mostly to guys, who could picture themselves tooling around town in a red 'Vette, a beautiful babe with sunglasses and windblown hair seated next to them.

I didn't really think I'd win the car. Linda must have sold hundreds of tickets, and all the kids at St. Rose of Sharon would be selling them too. At a buck a pop, who could resist taking a chance?

So I was kind of surprised when she came over a week after New Year's to tell me I'd won a prize.

"The Corvette!"

"No," she said, with a rueful little smile.

"The giant TV?"

She shook her head.

I tried to remember what the rest of the prizes were. "Linda, don't keep me in suspense," I begged. "What did I win?"

"A toaster!"

"A toaster?"

"With extra-wide slots so you can toast bagels," she said excitedly. "Isn't that *great*?"

She seemed so happy for me, I didn't want to burst her bubble. But it was hard to get worked up about a toaster. Even one with extra-wide slots.

"Who won the Corvette?" I asked.

"I think someone in Newburgh," she said. "I'm not sure."

"When do I get the toaster?" I asked glumly.

"They're holding it for you at the school," she said. "I'll pick it up next weekend."

"You don't have to," I said. "I can pick it up myself."

"No, no!" she said sharply. "I'll get it."

I must have looked startled, because she added hastily, "It'll give me a chance to see some of my old friends again."

"I'll go with you, then," I offered. "I can meet some of your fr—"

She slid her fingers into my hair, then trailed her thumb over my bottom lip. "Let's not talk about it now," she whispered.

So we didn't.

I forgot about the toaster until the following Sunday, when Linda brought it over. She even brought a bag of bagels with her and insisted on toasting us each a bagel so we could see how great the extra-wide slots were.

"It's the best bagel I ever ate," I said.

"Delicious," my mother agreed, considerately standing in front of our own toaster so Linda couldn't see it.

"Who did you say won the car?" Matt asked.

After Linda left, Matt came into the den, where I was watching a Knicks game. "Will, I have to talk to you."

"It's overtime," I said. "Three-point lead for the Bulls. Can't it wait?"

"It's about Linda."

Torn between the action on the screen and my brother's grave expression, I pressed the Mute button but kept my eye on the TV.

"Isn't she sweet?" I said, then groaned as Chicago scored a three-pointer. "Bringing the bagels and all."

"Well . . ." Matt hesitated. "Maybe not."

"What?"

The Knicks called a time-out. I turned my full attention to Matt. "What are you talking about?"

"There's no such school as St. Rose of Sharon," Matt said. "I looked it up."

"But there has to be," I said. "That's where Linda went before she moved here from . . . from . . ." I suddenly realized that I didn't know where the Shermans had lived before they moved to Cutter's Forge.

"Maybe they came from another state," I said. "If you only checked—"

"I checked every Catholic school in the country," Matt said.

"How did you do that?" I demanded.

"You can do anything with a computer," he answered. "And there is no school anywhere named St. Rose of Sharon. There's no *saint* named Rose of

Sharon. There's a St. Rose of Lima, but—"

"But my toaster!" I said. "What about my toaster? If I didn't win it in the raffle—"

"Anyone can buy a toaster," Matt said gently.

I slumped over on the couch, the Knicks game completely forgotten. "She lied?" I said. "Linda *lied*?"

"Will, she didn't just lie," Matt said. "She committed fraud. She broke the law. She must have collected hundreds of dollars for that fake charity. That's a crime."

"But the tickets," I said. "She had all those printed raffle tickets. How could she—"

"She probably printed them up herself. You can do anything with a computer," he repeated.

For the next week I was so dazed and confused, I didn't know whether to be furious with computers or with Linda. If it weren't for computers, Linda couldn't have pulled off her raffle scam. On the other hand, there were dishonest people long before there were computers, and if you were a dedicated con person, you could always find a way to sting the suckers.

I didn't know what to do. I didn't know what to say. I was torn between wanting to confront her with Matt's accusation and wanting everything to go on the way it had . . . the hand holding, the kissing, the adoring looks.

❤ ❤ ❤

Three weeks before Valentine's Day, she started dropping hints about the Sweetheart Stomp. I hadn't asked her to go, I hadn't talked about it—in fact, I'd hardly talked to her about anything.

"It'll be romantic, don't you think, Will?"

"I guess."

"Di Callahan asked if we wanted to double with her and her date—when she decides who to go with. And a whole bunch of people are going to Laugh Lines afterward. Doesn't that sound like fun?"

"Yeah."

"But I had to tell her I didn't even know if I'd be at the dance," Linda went on, her (moist, ripe) lips forming a pout. "I told her you hadn't asked me yet."

"Linda, I—" I almost worked up the courage to ask her if she'd lied—about the raffle, about her school, about her whole past life. She took my hand and pressed it against her cheek.

"Will, what *is* it? You've hardly spoken to me for days. Did I do something wrong?"

The touch of her hand, the catch in her voice, the fluttering of her eyelashes—suddenly I was jelly. I felt weak in the knees and light in the head. I pictured us at the dance, drifting around the floor, arms around each other, her sweet-smelling hair brushing against my mouth.

I forgot that I hate to dance. I forgot the Clean, Green Investment Club. I forgot that there was no St. Rose of Sharon. I forgot that this adorable creature next to me was possibly the slickest operator east of the Rockies.

And every doubt, every suspicion that had floated through my mind, was swept away.

Until three days later.

"Look what I saw on the bulletin board!" Linda handed me a piece of paper from a pile she'd carried into the lunchroom.

"The school bulletin board?"

"No, on the computer."

I sat down next to her, examined my tray, saw that the frankfurters were pale gray and the french fries pale white, and decided lunch could wait. I scanned the computer-printed announcement.

"**HAVE A HEART!**" read the headline. Then, in smaller type:

LITTLE BILLY THIGPEN OF BOISE, MONTANA, HAS ONLY TWO WISHES FOR VALENTINE'S DAY. HE WANTS TO GET WELL, AND HE WANTS TO MAKE THE *GUINNESS BOOK OF RECORDS*.

Little Billy, who's only nine years old, suffers from a rare and mysterious condition that

prevents him from properly metabolizing fats.

Most people want to cut down on fatty food—but Billy's problem is just the opposite. He needs enormous amounts of rich foods every day just to STAY AWAKE!

Billy's daily diet requires almost half a pound of butter, a quart of heavy cream, half a pound of bacon, three servings of ice cream, eight ounces of cheese, and as much red meat as he can swallow. Plus bologna, sausage, mayonnaise and rich, creamy desserts.

THE THIGPENS' FOOD BILL IS HUGE!!! They don't know how they're going to pay for Billy's groceries till he's sixteen, which is how long the doctors say he has to stay on the high-fat diet.

Without high-fat foods, Billy becomes weak and listless. He can't go to school or play with his little friends, or even concentrate on his homework. He could even go into a COMA!

Billy's parents, Marge and Vern, are too proud to ask for charity, but we FRIENDS OF LITTLE BILLY have come up with a way you can help.

Billy is dreaming of getting listed in the

Guinness Book of Records. **If everyone who reads this sends him a Valentine's Day card, and a donation of** *any amount you can afford, no matter how small,* **Billy could set a record for receiving the MOST VALENTINES OF ANYONE IN THE WORLD and maybe even get enough money to MAKE HIM WELL!!**

    Send your Valentines and donations to LITTLE BILLY'S HAVE A HEART FUND, P.O. BOX . . .

    I looked up at Linda. "I thought he lived in Montana."

    "He does."

    "Then why is the post office box in Cutter's Forge?" I asked.

    "Because I'm the local chairman of the fund," Linda said proudly.

    I didn't think to ask how she'd been selected for the honor. "But why can't people just send the money directly to Billy?"

    "The committee wanted all the cards to arrive at once, on Valentine's Day," Linda said. "If they just trickle in one at a time, it won't make as much of an impact. Think of Little Billy's face when the mailman comes on Valentine's Day with sacks and sacks of cards!"

    "You saw this on the computer?" I asked. "How do

you know it's legitimate? What if it's a fraud and there really isn't any Billy Thigpen?"

Her eyes grew wide. She shook her head and made *tsk*ing sounds. "Oh, Will, how can you be so cynical? What kind of a person would fake a tragic story like that?"

She went off to distribute the Have a Heart flyers around the cafeteria. I started to crumple mine up, then thought better of it. I stuck it in my notebook.

Even if my lunch had been edible, I couldn't have eaten it.

I had a heart . . . and it was breaking.

"I could be wrong," I said to Matt that night. God knows I wanted to be wrong. "Maybe I *am* too cynical."

"You never used to be," Matt said. "Until you met her." He examined the flyer for the Have a Heart Fund. "She said she got this off her computer?"

"Yeah." I had a sudden, hopeful thought. "Maybe it *is* a scam," I suggested, "but not hers. I mean, maybe someone else made up Little Billy. Maybe she's being conned, just like everyone else."

"But the cards and the money are going to her post office box," Matt pointed out. "If you were pulling something like this, would you trust someone else to collect the money?"

I slumped in my chair until I nearly slid to the floor. "It could be real," I said. "Just because the raffle was *maybe* phony doesn't mean this is.

"Or maybe she feels guilty about the raffle," I went on. "So she's throwing herself into this Have a Heart thing to try and make up for it."

I wanted so desperately to believe in Linda, to believe that she was basically good.

Matt wrinkled his forehead. "How is she in geography?"

"What? I don't know. What difference does it make?"

He pointed to the first paragraph of the flyer. "Look at this. Boise, Montana? Boise's not in Montana; it's in Idaho." He folded the paper into a glider and it skimmed across the room.

"I never noticed." I put my head in my hands.

"It's a good thing the money's going to Cutter's Forge," Matt said. "Because the post office is never going to find Boise, Montana."

My heart may have been broken, but it refused to lie down and play dead. What was this uncanny power Linda had over me, that I forgot her dishonesty every time she touched my cheek or leaned her head against my shoulder?

I knew perfectly well what it was.

But I seemed helpless to fight it.

A week before the Sweetheart Stomp, Linda invited me to have dinner at her house.

This was the first time I had been with her parents for more than a brief exchange of greetings. I felt so torn between love and distrust that it took me a while to realize that her mother and father were more tense than I was.

Mr. Sherman and I did the dishes after we cleared the table. Linda flitted in and out of the kitchen as if (to my cynical, suspicious mind) she wanted to keep tabs on our conversation.

"I'm glad Linda has a friend like you, Will," her father said. He didn't look at me but concentrated on Brillo-ing a stubborn scorch on the roasting pan.

"Yeah, well," I said intelligently.

"Sometimes I worry about her," he muttered.

I looked up, shaken, from the dishwasher, where I was trying to arrange plates in size order. "You do?"

He cleared his throat. He still didn't look at me. "She gets an ample allowance," he said.

"Huh?"

At which point Linda did one of her flits into the kitchen. She threw her arms around her father and gave him a big kiss on the cheek.

"You're working poor Will like a *slave*," she said. "He's supposed to be a guest."

"I don't mind," I said.

She ruffled her father's hair. "Isn't he sweet?" I didn't know if she was talking about him or me. I think maybe he didn't know either. Because when she flitted out of the kitchen, he finally looked up from the roasting pan, a strange expression on his face.

"She's a charming girl, isn't she?" He looked as powerless to resist Linda as I was.

I nodded. "Yes. Charming."

"But don't," he said, "give her any money."

The Saturday before Valentine's Day, Linda phoned. "I have to talk to you!" she whispered urgently.

"What's wrong?"

"Not on the phone! I'll be right over."

Ten minutes later she was pounding on our front door.

She practically dragged me into the den. I'd never seen her so frantic. I'd never seen her frantic at all.

She handed me a piece of paper.

"What's this?" I asked.

"Read it," she ordered. "Oh, Will, I don't know what to do!"

At the top of the page was printed: ANTHONY J. PALERMO, ATTORNEY-AT-LAW. The letter read:

Dear Ms. Sherman:

It has come to our attention that you are representing yourself as an agent for William (Little Billy) Thigpen's "Have a Heart" Fund.

You should know that no one except myself and Vern and Marge Thigpen, William's parents, are authorized to receive money in Billy's name.

Therefore, we are asking you to immediately cease and desist from any fund-raising or solicitation on behalf of Billy, and to forward any monies and greeting cards you have already collected to us at . . .

There was a Bozeman, Montana, address, and the letter was signed *Anthony J. Palermo, Esq.*

I handed her back the letter.

"What's going on?" I asked. "I thought you were the local chairman of the Little Billy fund."

"I don't know what's going on," she said tearfully. She looked around the den, as if to make sure no one could hear us. Then she leaned close to me and said,

"Will, there is no Little Billy fund. There's no Little Billy. *I made him up.*"

"You made him up?" I can't say I was shocked. But I was as miserable as I had ever been in my life. Up till now I guess I had somehow hoped I was wrong, that Matt was wrong, and that Linda's father was just . . . cautious.

"What are you saying?" I demanded.

"It was only a . . . joke." Linda clasped my hand tightly. "I made up Little Billy. I got the idea from a story in the *World Wide Weekly* about this kid who had to eat a high-fat diet. But he was from Italy. His name wasn't Billy Thigpen. I didn't think anyone's name was Billy Thigpen."

"Oh, Linda. How could you? Why did you?"

"I told you," she said impatiently. "It was just a joke. You know, a computer thing. I wanted to see how many valentines I could collect."

"And the money you raised?" I reminded her. "I think money is key here."

"I'll bet you're right." She nodded. "They probably don't care a hoot about the valentines. What am I going to *do*?"

"I think you'd better send them everything," I said. "They've hired a lawyer, and they know your address. . . ."

"It's not fair!" she sulked. "I dream up a kid and the kid turns out to be real, with the *exact* rare disease I give him? I mean, what are the odds?"

I guess that was the moment the spell was finally broken, when Linda acted as if she were the victim instead of the perpetrator. The only regret she had was that she'd gotten caught.

She frowned. Her lips turned down, and her eyes were hot with anger. She clenched her fists as if she wanted to punch someone.

I knew just how she felt.

She hadn't collected too much money; only about three hundred dollars. I figured she'd made as much, or more, from the raffle.

Matt deleted the Palermo letterhead from his computer. We wouldn't need it anymore. Anthony Palermo, Matt's friend at Montana State University, sent the package of checks, cash, and cards back to us as soon as he received it.

I tore up the checks and donated the cash to the American Cardiac Association.

I sent all the valentines to Linda.

"You see?" Matt said triumphantly. "You can do anything with a computer."

Yeah.

Except mend a broken heart.

Metamorphosis

I got the idea at Cloris Ackerman's birthday party. It was a sleepover. She'd finished opening all her presents. We'd scraped up the salsa and guacamole with the last fragments of taco chips, and it was only one A.M.—way too early to go to sleep.

We'd spent a wonderful hour dishing the girls who weren't there: weird Amy Porter, scheming Linda Sherman, insufferably blond Di Callahan.

Then, inevitably, we turned our attention to boys. Cloris started a game of "Which would you rather?"

"Okay," she said. "Which would you rather: kiss Batso Batkowski, or wet your finger and stick it in a light socket?"

There was a small chorus of *"Eeuww"*s. But a clear majority chose kissing Batso over electrocution.

"I've got one," Andi Fallows said. "Which would you rather: eat sheep's eyes, or hold hands with Robert La Motte?"

"That's *awful!*" Cloris said. "What a choice."

"That's the whole point of the game, isn't it?" Andi retorted. "If it was easy, we wouldn't want to play."

"But Robert La Motte." Cloris groaned. "He's so pathetic."

He *was* pathetic. He was short, thin, clumsy, and shy. He tripped over chairs, stumbled into walls, and dropped cafeteria trays onto people's laps.

He mumbled—mostly "Sorry," or "Oops," or "Ouch." As far as I knew, he never worked up the courage to talk to a girl—or even look one in the eye. He wasn't particularly smart. He certainly wasn't athletic. In fact, he seemed to have absolutely no talent for anything except tripping, stumbling, and spilling his lunch.

His clothes—flannel shirts in ugly plaids and saggy corduroy pants—looked as if he'd fished them out of a Goodwill bin. In the dark.

"I feel sorry for him," I said.

"So you'd hold hands with him, Kate?" Andi asked.

"I didn't say that."

"How bad could sheep's eyes be?" Laurel Baker said. "In some countries, they're considered delicacies."

"We don't live in any of those countries," Cloris pointed out. "God bless America."

"Does anyone know," B.J. Green asked, "what headcheese is, actually? Or blood pudding? Or toad-in-the-hole?"

"What?" Everyone turned to stare at her. She was lying on her stomach, hands under her chin.

"What's headcheese got to do with anything?" Andi asked.

"Oh, you know. Just icky-sounding stuff people eat. Eyes, heads, toads, blood. I mean, headcheese can't really be made of heads, can it?"

"I never cease to be amazed at the way your mind works," Andi said. "We were talking about Robert La Motte."

"And comparing him to icky stuff," B.J. said. "Well, I agree with Kate. I feel sorry for him too."

"Okay, fine," Andi said. "So you'd rather hold hands with him than eat sheep's eyes."

"I'd rather harness this energy for the good of mankind!" B.J. shot back.

"Humankind," Cloris corrected. "And what are you *talking* about?"

"We've spent the whole night gossiping about people," B.J. said, "and thinking up sarcastic cracks. If we put that kind of effort into something *constructive*—"

"Give me a break, B.J.!" Cloris said. "This is a

party, not a conference on world peace."

"Think globally, act locally," B.J. said.

"What does *that* mean?" Cloris asked.

"World peace starts at home," B.J. replied.

Andi crawled into her sleeping bag and zipped it up to her neck. "Good night," she said. "This party has taken a very boring turn."

"No, wait!" I said. "I have an idea."

"Whatever it is, I'll donate ten dollars if we stop talking about this," Andi said.

"It won't take any money," I said excitedly. "Well, no more than a couple of dollars. And it'll be fun."

"What is it?" B.J. asked.

"All Robert La Motte needs," I said, "is a little self-confidence."

"Oh, yeah," Cloris said drily. "A little self-confidence and a bodybuilding course and public-speaking lessons and a complete makeover."

"We have to start somewhere," I said.

"We have to start *what* somewhere?" Andi asked. "And why do *we* have to start it?"

"Listen," I said, "we all agree that Robert is pathetic and needs help, right?"

"He's pathetic," Cloris said. "But why do *we* want to help him?"

"Cloris, where's your heart?" B.J. cried. "Where's your *compassion*?" She sat up and turned toward me. "I want to help him," she declared. "What's your idea?"

"If he thinks people like him," I said, "he might not be so shy. He might be able to talk to girls without mumbling and falling over things."

"What girls would want to talk to *him*?" Andi asked.

"All the girls who send him valentines!" I said.

"Are you serious?" Cloris said. "Who's going to send Robert La Motte a valentine?"

"We are," I said. "Every one of us."

"Are you *mad*?" Andi shrieked. "You want Robert La Motte to think I *like* him?"

"You don't have to sign your name," I said. "That's the beauty of the thing. As long as he gets a lot of cards, he's going to feel good. And if they're from 'A Secret Admirer' or something like that, he can imagine anyone he wants having a crush on him."

"That's a great idea!" B.J. said. "We could change his whole life!"

"And they don't have to be mushy," I added. "They can be like, 'For a Special Friend,' or 'Thinking of You.' We just want him to know people like him."

"But people *don't* like him," Andi argued.

"But if he thinks they do," I said, "he'll feel good about himself. He'll have a better self-image."

"He doesn't deserve a better self-image," Andi said. "He's creepy."

"That is *so* cruel," B.J. scolded. "What if no one liked *you*? What if people thought *you* were creepy? Can't you put yourself in Robert's place?"

"No." Andi said. "I can't even put myself in the same room with him."

But everyone finally agreed that sending valentines to Robert La Motte could do no harm, and might actually do him some good. Cloris thought that, if nothing else, it would be an interesting experiment in human psychology.

So the next morning the eight of us trooped down to the Hallmark store and bought valentines for Robert La Motte.

"Don't you think," B.J. said, as we walked back to Cloris's, "that it would be more effective if a couple of us signed our real names?"

"Oh, no!" Cloris said. "That wasn't the deal."

"Yes, but if he actually knows that some *real* girls wanted to—"

Andi whirled around and waved her Hallmark bag under B.J.'s nose. "Real girls *don't* want to!" she snapped. "That's why we're doing it!"

But I thought B.J. was right. The whole project would be more successful if Robert got a few cards from people he knew.

Which is why I felt compelled to sign mine. After all, it *was* my idea.

The card wasn't the least bit romantic.

> *You're a very nice person,*
> *And I just want to say*
> *I'm thinking of you*
> *This Valentine's Day.*

How could he possibly read anything more than polite friendliness into that sentiment? B.J. said she'd sign her card, and Laurel almost promised she would, too. So it wasn't as if my valentine would stand out among the other seven as a blazing declaration of love.

It certainly wouldn't incite Robert to hit on me. Robert wouldn't know how to hit on *anyone*. Trip over them, maybe, but hit on them? Never.

I couldn't wait to see Robert after the cards arrived. I tried not to hope that he'd be transformed from a shambling klutz to a suave, self-assured stud. I told myself not to expect too much. I told myself eight valentines could not turn Robert La Motte into Mr. Wonderful.

I was wrong.

Two days before Valentine's Day, Robert La Motte swaggered into homeroom like a lord visiting his subjects.

It was astonishing. He didn't trip over any chairs. He held his head high and surveyed the room as if it were his kingdom.

B.J. leaned over. "Am I imagining it," she whispered, "or does he look—"

"I don't think you're imagining it," I whispered back.

"He's a new person," B.J. said. "We did *good.*"

"I guess we must have." I gazed at Robert and tried not to feel too smug, but it was hard. I'd never changed anyone's life before. This was, I told myself, a tremendous accomplishment. It's not everyone who can say, "I made a difference." But I had. Robert La Motte was positively oozing self-confidence, and it was all my doing.

"Hey, Kate," Robert said, as we headed out of homeroom to our first class.

"Hey, Robert." I tried not to show surprise at his greeting.

"Thanks for your card. I never realized you had the hots for me."

"Excuse me?"

"Oh, come on, Katie. Don't be coy. Actions speak louder than words."

"What actions?" I asked. "I just sent you a nice friendly card. You're reading too much into it."

"I'm reading between the lines," he said, practically leering at me. "I know what you really wanted to say."

"No, you don't!" I said it so loudly that kids in the hallway turned to stare at me. What had gotten into him? How could he have possibly misinterpreted my good deed?

"Then why did you send me a card?" he asked. His voice was patient, as if he were reasoning with a three-year-old.

"Because . . . because . . ." I couldn't tell him the real reason. I couldn't tell him it was because I felt sorry for him.

That would undo all the good work we had done. If Robert had miraculously developed self-confidence as a result of our valentines, how could I snatch that away?

"I got a whole batch of cards," he said proudly. "But yours meant the most. So what I thought," he went on, "is that maybe we could get together and—"

"*No!*"

"What do you mean, no?"

"I mean *no*. I mean sending that card was just a friendly gesture."

"Well, I'd like to show you"—he lowered his voice—"some *real* friendly gestures."

I shuddered in disgust as he leaned too close to me. I backed away and found myself smack up against a row of lockers.

"Robert, I don't want to see any of your friendly gestures." My voice was shrill with panic. "I just sent you a card because . . ."

"You think you're the only one who sent me a valentine?" he sneered. "You think *you're* the best I can do?"

"*What?*"

"I've got plenty of babes to choose from." He folded his arms across his chest and glared at me.

"Babes?" I repeated. How could eight greeting cards cause such a complete reversal of personality? All I'd wanted was to give Robert a little self-esteem. But something had gone horribly wrong.

"What's gotten into you?" I demanded. "You're acting like an idiot."

He spun on his heel and started down the hall. "The worm has turned, sugar," he said. "Eat your heart out."

"Worm!" I shouted after him. "The key word is *worm!*"

"We've created a Frankenstein," Cloris declared.

"You mean a Frankenstein's monster," B.J. corrected. "Frankenstein was the—"

"Oh, B.J., *please!*" Cloris snapped. "Do you always have to be so literal? The thing is, what are we going to do about him?"

We were in Andi's room that afternoon, the same eight of us who had been at Cloris's sleepover.

"What do you mean, 'we'?" Andi snarled. "It was Kate's brilliant idea."

"Well, it's everybody's problem now," Cloris said. "He's hit on half the girls in school."

"But he's struck out with every one of them," I said. "By tomorrow he'll run out of girls to hit on. I don't see why this is our problem."

"What makes you think he'll stop?" Cloris yelled. "He's out of control! He might just go back to his first choice and start all over again."

That would be me. "Oh, no."

"If he's rejected enough times," B.J. suggested, "maybe he'll eventually get the message." She looked troubled. "But I feel kind of guilty about this. I mean, we did want him to think that a whole bunch of girls liked him. Now we're trying to shoot him down. It doesn't seem right."

"Is it our fault he turned into an obnoxious boor?" Cloris demanded. "All we did was send him some valentines. It's not our fault he turned into Dr. Jekyll."

"Actually," B.J. began, "it was Mr. Hyde who—"

"B.J., *I don't care!*" Cloris cut in. "All I know is that the only thing worse than the old Robert La Motte is the new Robert La Motte."

"It *is* a frightening personality change," B.J. said soberly.

"So, we all agree," Andi said. "Kate has to do something."

"Aw, c'mon, guys," I pleaded. "What am I going to do?"

"Maybe you should tell him the truth," Laurel said. "Or part of the truth. I mean, you don't have to tell him we thought he was pathetic. Just say we were trying to boost his self-confidence."

"I don't know," said B.J. unhappily. "It doesn't

seem right to build up someone's self-confidence and then tear it down again."

"Fine," Cloris said. "Then *you* go out with him, and maybe he'll leave the rest of us alone."

"He probably has some good qualities," B.J. said. "Everybody does."

"No doubt," Cloris agreed. "Tell us about them after your date."

"All right, all right," I said finally. "It was my idea, and a person has to accept responsibility for her actions. I'll talk to him tomorrow."

"What are you going to say?" Laurel asked.

I sighed. "I don't know. Some version of the truth."

"Try not to hurt his feelings," B.J. urged. "We don't want him to get all shy and klutzy again."

"Speak for yourself," Andi retorted.

I hardly slept that night. I dreaded facing Robert. I was consumed with guilt that my good intentions had led him so wildly astray.

What could I tell him? How could I explain that none of his valentines were from people who really liked him?

Would he listen to anything I said? After all, his last, bitter words to me were "You think *you're* the best I can do?"

I tossed and turned, trying to come up with alternatives to the truth. Maybe I could just *pretend* I'd talked to him. How would Cloris and B.J. and the others know whether I had or not? No, I couldn't deal in deception anymore. It was just too tiring.

I spent most of the night rehearsing gentle, non-insulting ways to tell Robert La Motte the only reason he got eight valentines was that we felt sorry for him. That no one who sent him a card really wanted anything to do with him. And in short, uneasy spurts, I dreamed of Robert, crumbling, like decaying plaster, at the cruel truth.

I was bleary-eyed when I got to school the next day.

I sagged against my locker, trying to remember the combination, then trying to remember what it was I'd wanted to put in or take out of it.

I was so woozy that Robert must have been standing next to me for several minutes before I realized he was there.

"Just the person I wanted to see," I said. If I *could* see.

"Really?" he replied. "Yesterday you didn't want to look at me."

"I have to talk to you," I began. I didn't give myself a chance to chicken out. "I wanted to explain . . ."

"Robert," a sweet voice cooed. "There you are."

Mimi Ostermeyer slid herself between us and whispered something into Robert's ear. He grinned, nodded, and gently brushed a stray curl off her forehead.

I'm hallucinating, I thought. *Or maybe I'm not in school at all. Maybe I'm still at home in bed, dreaming this impossible scenario.*

I shook my head and rubbed my eyes. When I opened them, I was still in school, and Robert and Mimi had their arms around each other's waists. They were on the verge of outright smooching.

My head spun. Everything I thought I knew about love and psychology, human relationships, and the way the world worked was completely upside down.

Mimi was a perfectly normal, attractive girl, and a talented cellist. What could she possibly want with Robert La Motte?

"It's a miracle," I muttered.

They tore themselves away from each other for a moment.

"Kate?" Mimi asked. "Did you say something?"

"Kate wants to talk to me," Robert said smoothly. He squeezed Mimi's hand. "I'll meet you in front of English, okay?"

"Don't be too long," she whispered shyly.

Robert watched her walk off down the hall. "Great

little gal," he remarked. "Not my usual type, but great little gal."

"Type?" I blurted out. "You have a *type*?"

He eyed me none too fondly. "You wanted to talk to me?"

"I did?"

He drummed his fingers against my locker impatiently. "Yes, you did. So what did you want to say?"

"Um . . . well, I only . . ." I stammered.

"Mimi's waiting for me," he said.

Why? I wanted to ask. *How?* How could our eight valentines have made such an impact?

"I just wanted to wish you Happy Valentine's Day," I said finally.

"Well . . . thanks." He seemed surprised. "No hard feelings? I mean, you did get the first shot at me."

"No hard feelings," I said quickly. "You and Mimi are perfect for each other." What a whopper—but at this point, what was one more insincere comment?

"She must think so, too," he said with a smug little grin. "Or she'd never have sent me that valentine."

He strode off down the hall, jauntily, hands in his pockets. He didn't even trip over his untied shoelace.

Two Coins in the Fountain

*T*here is a legend about the fountain of Cupid in front of Antonelli's Ristorante and Pizzeria on Main Street in downtown Cutter's Forge.

It is said that if you turn your back and toss a coin over your shoulder into the fountain, whatever you wish for will come true.

Many customers toss coins into the green cement fountain, and many dip into the fountain for quarters to feed the parking meters that line Main Street. Those who fish coins out of the fountain probably aren't making wishes—unless they wish that none of the Antonellis would catch them filching quarters.

No one knows for sure how many people have had their wishes granted. But a week before Valentine's Day, B.J. Green was convinced that nothing short of magic could rescue her from the prospect of a very depressing February 14th.

She'd get a card from her parents—she always did. And she'd get a card that her little sister, Megan, had made in school with lots of lopsided hearts and crooked daisies on the front. They were sweet cards, and B.J. appreciated them. But she already knew her parents and sister loved her.

She wanted a valentine from someone else. Someone she wasn't related to. Someone who did not love her like a sister, or a daughter. Someone who loved her with a burning flame of passion, someone who couldn't live without her, someone who went weak-kneed at the very sight of her.

And she wanted to go to the Valentine's Day dance at school. Not that she loved dancing so much. In fact, she hardly ever got to do it, except when she practiced new moves with her girl friends.

But the point of going to the Sweetheart Stomp wasn't simply to dance. The point was, she wanted . . . *needed* . . . an evening of stardust and romance with a boy who thought she was wonderful.

As far as B.J. knew, nobody (except her sister and her parents) thought she was wonderful. As far as B.J. knew, everyone thought she was perfectly ordinary. She had no outstanding qualities whatsoever. She wasn't heartbreakingly beautiful, she didn't excel in any sport or subject, she was completely inept at flirting and too shy to strike up a conversation with a boy she would have liked to know better.

I'm hopeless, she told herself. *If I were a boy, I wouldn't be interested in me either.*

But a week before Valentine's Day, B.J. stood in front of the fountain at Antonelli's, glumly chewing a piece of mushroom-and-onion pizza and gazing at the coins in the pool at Cupid's feet.

She had received a quarter and a dime in change when she'd bought her pizza. She fingered the coins and wondered if any of the wishes made at Antonelli's fountain had ever come true.

Immediately she scolded herself for being a superstitious, gullible fool. Then she thought, *But after all, what can you buy with thirty-five cents?*

A pack of chewing gum. Or a newspaper. She'd already read this morning's paper. And she wasn't a gum chewer.

It couldn't hurt, B.J. thought. *The worst that can happen is I blow thirty-five cents.*

She fished the quarter from her pocket, turned around, and threw it over her shoulder into the fountain. "I wish someone would ask me to the Sweetheart Stomp," she whispered.

A snappy red Miata convertible slipped into the only available parking space in front of the restaurant. Derek Hofstader hopped out of the car without bothering to open the door.

"B.J. Green," he said, walking straight toward her. "Just the girl I wanted to see."

B.J.'s mouth dropped open. She closed it. She could still taste the onions from her pizza. It was hard not to show her surprise. Why would Derek Hofstader want to see her?

"Me?" she repeated.

"Yes, indeed," he said smoothly. Everything about Derek was smooth. And why not? He was gorgeous, athletic, and rich. He practically oozed self-confidence. And why not? He'd always had everything, including any girl he ever wanted. At the moment, he was going out with Di Callahan.

So what did he want with B.J.?

"I know it's pretty short notice," he said, "but would you like to go to the Sweetheart Stomp with me?"

B.J. was so stunned, she couldn't answer. Derek had never shown the slightest interest in her. She would never expect him to.

"I . . . I . . ." She tried not to stammer.

"I know it's sudden," Derek said. He put his hand

on her shoulder. "But I've had my eye on you for a long time."

She felt his hand almost burning through her jacket. "I thought you and Di—"

"Ancient history," he cut in. "You're the one I really wanted."

Wow! thought B.J. *That fountain works fast.*

"Well . . . sure."

"Great!" Derek gave her shoulder a little squeeze. B.J. tried not to faint. "I'll pick you up at seven."

Seven, B.J. thought, dazed. *That gives me a week and four hours to buy a dress, get shoes, find out how Amy Porter does her nails, and learn to talk without stammering.*

The week and four hours went by in a blur. B.J. felt as if time had somehow been compressed, and that only minutes had elapsed between the moment she threw her quarter into the fountain and Derek came to pick her up for the dance.

She'd bought a midnight-blue dress, and dark-blue heels with T-straps, and she'd had her nails done in a pearly white polish at Sofronia's Nail Salon, where Amy Porter had sent her.

"You look *beautiful.*" Megan's eyes were wide as B.J. came down the stairs.

"No, I don't," B.J. said self-consciously.

"You *do*," Megan insisted.

Derek picked her up at seven. "There's a little predance get-together at Di's," he said. "Why don't we drop in there first?"

"Okay." *Anything you say,* B.J. thought. *This is going to be the most romantic night of my life. This is going to be the* only *romantic night of my life.*

But it wasn't that okay. At Di's, Derek hovered over B.J. like a mother robin with a nestling. He made sure she had soda and chips, and when he wasn't feeding her, he kept his arm draped possessively over her shoulder. Especially when Di was watching.

At the dance Derek was not so attentive. During slow numbers B.J. thrilled to the feel of him holding her close. But she had the uneasy impression that even while he was humming into her ear, he was searching the gym for Diana.

When they were doing fast dances, B.J. could see Derek's face. And she knew that Derek was not really seeing her.

And somehow, wherever they started out on the dance floor, they always seemed to end up right next to Di and her date.

It was supposed to be the most romantic night of

her life, but B.J. was growing more and more uncomfortable. She tried to tell herself that she was imagining things, but she knew she wasn't. She tried to tell herself to just relax and enjoy the moment, that whatever was going on between Derek and Diana needn't affect her. All she'd wished for was to go to the Sweetheart Stomp, and here she was. She'd never expected to marry Derek Hofstader; she'd never even expected to date him. She'd only wanted one magical evening, and she'd gotten one. It just wasn't as magical as she'd hoped.

Near ten o'clock Derek excused himself to visit the bathroom, and B.J. wandered over to the refreshment table. She looked around for Diana but didn't see her. B.J. tried not to be suspicious—but she couldn't help it.

She was pouring herself a glass of punch when she heard Cloris's voice. Cloris was whispering something to Andi Fallows. B.J. could make out only a few words.

". . . poor B.J. . . . just to get back at Di . . . rotten thing to do . . ."

She turned around.

"B.J.!" Cloris looked stricken. She tried to say something else, but for the first time since B.J. had known her, Cloris was speechless.

"It's true, then?" B.J. said. "Derek just wanted to make Diana jealous?"

Andi couldn't look at her. "He said he was going to ask the first girl he saw. That must have been you."

"Andi!" Cloris snapped at her. "Why did you tell her?"

"She has a right to know what a rat he is."

B.J. felt as if her insides were shriveling. The paper cup slipped between her fingers and bounced on the table. She watched as the punch splattered a large ruby stain across the white paper tablecloth.

She couldn't look at Cloris. She couldn't look at Andi. She couldn't look at anyone. She just stared at the spreading stain and wished she could disappear.

B.J. stood in front of the fountain at Antonelli's, glumly chewing a piece of mushroom-and-onion pizza.

"Where . . . how . . . ?" She whirled around, trying to figure out what had happened. A moment ago, she'd been at the Sweetheart Stomp spilling punch and wishing she could disappear.

Had a whole week passed? Was Valentine's Day over? Had her wish come true? Had any of it really happened?

B.J. reached into her pocket. Only a dime remained. That meant she had used the quarter for a wish—and the wish had been granted!

The fountain worked! It really worked! Even if her wish hadn't turned out very well, it *had* come true.

A policewoman strolled toward her, carrying a ticket book and checking the parking meters.

"What day is it?" B.J. asked her.

The policewoman eyed her suspiciously. "Saturday."

"No, I mean the date."

"February seventh. Are you all right? What's your name? Do you know your address?"

"I'm fine, just fine." B.J. breathed a sigh of relief. She wasn't sure what was happening, but it seemed as if her wish had come true only in a *possible* future. Like a tryout, B.J. thought. A practice wish. Sort of a warning to be careful what you wish for.

Whatever had happened, the key thing was that the fountain did grant wishes. And she still had a dime left. She could make another wish. This time, she would be more careful.

She turned her back and threw the dime over her shoulder into the fountain. The policewoman watched her curiously.

"I wish," B.J. whispered, "to go to the dance with someone who *really* likes me."

❤ ❤ ❤

She was in the center of the gym. Heart-shaped balloons floated overhead. The band, Yellow Fever, was playing "Love Me Tender." Badly.

Robert La Motte was nibbling on her fingertips.

B.J. screamed.

"Oops, sorry," Robert said. "Did I bite you?"

B.J. stared at him. He was wearing a tuxedo. Badly. Part of his shirt hung over his electric-blue cummerbund. His matching bow tie was half undone. Little beads of sweat dotted the trace of mustache hairs on his upper lip.

"You are everything I ever dreamed of in a woman," he said ardently.

You are my worst nightmare! B.J. wanted to scream. How had this happened?

"Stop chewing on my fingers!" she ordered. "People are watching."

"I know," he murmured, pulling her close. "I wish we were alone, too. Ever since I got your valentine . . ."

B.J. tried to unwrap his arms from her waist. But for some inexplicable reason, Yellow Fever suddenly began playing a tango.

Robert La Motte, his soul apparently inflamed by the tempestuous Latin rhythm, spun B.J. around the center of the floor. He yanked her back and began to tango.

He loped across the gym, dragging her with him. He whirled and galloped in the opposite direction. B.J. tried to break free, but he had her in a death grip, and all she could do was sprint along with him, as her classmates clapped and cheered and hooted.

"This is *humiliating!*" she shouted into his ear.

He didn't hear her. At least, he didn't hear her correctly. "Exhilarating, *yes!*" he cried. "To do the dance of love with the girl you love!"

"I don't love you!" B.J. screamed. "I don't know how I got here, but it's a mistake!"

"I love you too!" he shouted. "We can go for steak later!"

Whirling around the gym, B.J. got dizzier and dizzier. The whoops and jeers of her (former) friends grew in a deafening crescendo. They sounded like a swarm of killer bees.

She wouldn't have minded, she thought desperately, if this were happening with someone she loved. Then if people snickered or jeered, she would at least have the strength and conviction that she was with the person she was meant to be with. It wouldn't matter what anyone else thought.

But Robert La Motte?

"I wish I were dead!" she moaned.

"It does go to your head," Robert agreed. "The tango is the most passionate of dances!"

B.J. stood in front of Antonelli's Ristorante and Pizzeria. She was chewing on a piece of mushroom-and-onion pizza. She swallowed, turned around, and looked at the fountain.

Dazed, she felt in her pocket. The quarter and the dime were gone. She looked into the pool at Cupid's feet. Of course, she couldn't identify any individual coins, but she was sure her thirty-five cents were somewhere near Cupid's toes.

Good grief. Two coins, two wishes come true.

She shook her head. All along, she'd thought the legend of the fountain was only that—a legend, probably dreamed up by the Antonellis to generate some extra cash.

But the legend was no legend, and the fountain was no ordinary fountain. It had an awesome power.

B.J. couldn't move. The policewoman was still there, checking parking meters. It seemed as if no time at all had passed—and maybe it hadn't.

Two practice wishes? B.J. mused. Two possible futures? Two foretastes of what could happen if her wish was granted?

She had no idea how magic worked or if there was any scientific aspect to what she had just experienced. But she did know that in all the classic tales of magic, three wishes were pretty much standard. If this fountain had a three-wish limit, she still had one wish coming.

She searched her pockets again. Nothing. She'd had the thirty-five cents' change, and that was it. She hadn't brought her wallet with her. She'd taken only enough money for one piece of pizza.

I'll just go home and get another quarter, she thought. *And this time . . .*

And this time, what? she asked herself. *How can I be sure of making the right wish? What if you do only get three wishes, and you're stuck with the last one? What if the first two were rehearsals, and the third is permanent, with no do-overs?*

Yes, she longed for an evening of magic and romance. Yes, she wished for a boy who would think she was wonderful. Yes, she wanted to go to the Sweetheart Stomp.

But there are worse things than not having a date for a dance. There are worse things than being alone on Valentine's Day.

Your wishes could come true.

B.J. threw her pizza crust into a trash bin. She turned away from the fountain and started to walk toward home.

She looked up at the marquee of the Main Street Uniplex movie theater.

COMING FRIDAY: *VALENTINE'S DAY, PART VI: CUPID'S CARNAGE*!!

That's what I'll do on Valentine's Day, B.J. decided. *I'll take Megan to the movies.*

But maybe not this one.

Russian Overture

[From the Cutter's Forge
High School *Courier*]

Our Russian Friend, Alexei Grigorov
by Janushka Farrentino

Alexei Grigorov, a foreign exchange student from St. Petersburg, Russia, will be staying with the family of Teddy Klein this semester as he attends Cutter's Forge High School. Alexei, who has studied English since he was ten years old, hopes to be a biochemist or a chemical engineer one day.

He enjoys reading, dancing, and solving math puzzles. His favorite book is *Stranger in a Strange Land* by Robert Heinlein.

"What I like best about being in America," he says, "is opportunity to speak English. Communicating is hard at first. But I think every day I talk a little better."

"And sometimes"—Alexei smiles as he says this—"you do not need to talk at all."

Taped Interview of Alexei Grigorov
by Jamie Farrentino
Cassette #1, Side A

"Alexei, the school newspaper wanted me to interview you, to find out what it's like to be a foreign exchange student in America."

"Yes, *da*, I love America."

"I know Teddy was supposed to help us out here because he takes Russian and I don't, but he told me your English was so good that we wouldn't need any help."

"Teddy is funny dude."

"Yeah, right. Teddy's a regular riot."

"Teddy is at a riot? What does he protest? Why he does not ask me to riot also? I have never been to riot."

"No, no, there's no riot. I just meant—Teddy *is* a funny dude. Likes to play tricks on people."

"Yes, I love Trix. Also Lucky Charms."

"No, not that kind of tricks. I mean, like telling me we wouldn't have any problems communicating."

"I have not problems with Communists. I am not Communist. Some Russian peoples are Communist. But I have not much politics. Maybe why I am never in riot."

"I'm going to kill Teddy. He told me this would be a piece of cake."

"I have no cake. I have Twinkies. Do you wish Twinkies?"

"Alexei, listen to me. I have to write a story about you for the newspaper."

"Yes, yes, I am very proud."

"I don't speak *any* Russian."

"Is no problem. We speak in English."

"Ohhh-kay. I'll go very slowly. But I *will* kill Teddy when I see him again because I just *know* he thought it would be funny to have me try to do an interview with neither of us understanding the other. He's probably got a video camera hidden somewhere."

"You are speaking fast again. Please speak more slow."

"Okay. What . . . is . . . the . . . biggest . . ."

"You do not must speak *that* slow. I am not moron."

"Sorry. What's the biggest difference between American schools and Russian schools? Is it hard to be a stranger in a strange land?"

"Ah, good book! *Stranger in a Strange Land.* Robert Heinlein. Favorite book. I read three times, one time in English."

"Oh boy. All right, that's something. Let me make a note. Favorite book, *Stranger in a Strange Land.*"

"Is like me. Russian guy in America."

"Exactly! Now we're getting somewhere. How does it feel to be a Russian guy in America? I think I'd be awfully homesick if I went to Russia for six months."

"You come to Russia? You stay with me. Not six months maybe. Maybe two weeks. I show you around."

"Alexei, I don't think this is going to work without a translator. I'm sure it's my fault—well, it's really Teddy's fault—but I just don't seem to be able to make you understand me."

"You don't come to Russia?"

"No."

"Bummer. Teddy tell me you like."

"Teddy told you I like Russia? I've never been to Russia. That's just another of his—"

"No, no. Teddy tell me you like *me*."

"Teddy told you I— How could he— I mean, I never told— Wait till I get hold of that creep. He's going to be dog meat."

"I do not meet his dog. He does not have dog. It is not true?"

"What? Is what not true?"

"You do not like me?"

"Well, sure, I—I mean, you're very— I mean, all the girls think you're—"

"Your face gets red. I ask you a hard question?"

"*I'm* supposed to be asking the questions."

"This is America. Anyone can ask questions. Also can say, I take Fifth Amendment. So you don't must answer my question."

"*What* question? I've forgotten what the question was!"

"You are still red on your face. You really forget? I ask, do you like me? You answer. Or you say 'I take Fifth Amendment.'"

"I . . . um . . . take the Fifth Amendment."

"This easier in Russia. No Fifth Amendment. Okay, is your turn to ask questions again."

"Alexei, this is hopeless. We need Teddy or someone from Russian class to help translate. We just don't understand each other."

"I tell Teddy not to help translate."

"No, no, you've got it backward. You have to tell Teddy we *need* him to help."

"I do not be backward. Before you come, I tell Teddy buzz off."

"*What?* Teddy wanted to help with the interview?"

"Yes. So do not kill him. I tell him I want to be with you one-on-one. Is my idea. I tell him, two is company, three is a group."

"You wanted to be alone with me?"

"Fifth Amendment. But if you do not like me, I will tell Teddy to help with interview. Then *I* will kill him."

"Oh, Alexei."

"It's nice how you call my name. Soft. Like in romantic love movie. Is okay I call you Janushka?"

"Janushka? Instead of Jamie?"

"Is nickname. For someone you like. Should call you Jamushka, but sound like messy jelly. You have date for Valentine's dance?"

"No."

"You go with me? I'm good dancer. Do all American dances."

"Oh, Alexei, I'd love to go to the dance with you. I wouldn't care if you had two left feet."

"I would care. Too hard to find shoes."

"No, I meant—"

"That was joke. I have swell sense of humor. But funnier in Russian."

"It's funny in English, too."

"I make joke when nervous."

"You don't have to be nervous. It's just a little interview for the school newspaper."

"Not nervous about interview. Nervous to ask can I kiss you."

"Oh. Now *I'm* nervous."

"Maybe we finish interview. Get to know better. Then not be so nervous."

"That's a good idea. Okay, where were we?"

"Teddy's house."

"No, I mean—"

"Know what you mean. I make joke again. Hard to concentrate. I keep thinking about kissing."

"Me too. Umm, you know what? Maybe we should just . . . get the kissing out of the way, and then we can . . ."

[End of Interview]

Call Waiting

"Hi, Andi. It's me, Di. I was wondering if you and— Oops, can you hold a minute? I have another call. Thanks.

"Hello? Oh, Mark. Well, hello. Fine. Oh, nothing much. What's happening? The dance? Oh, how sweet of you to ask. But listen, I'm on the other line right now, so— Oh, definitely. Immediately. The moment I get off. 'Bye.

"Andi? I'm back. That was Mark Chetwin. He wanted to ask me to the Sweetheart Stomp. As if! *Quel nerve,* as they say in French. I put off Jason Glick and Warren— Oops, there it goes again. Hold on, okay?

"Hello? Adam, what a surprise. Oh, thanks. You really liked it? Yeah, it's new. No, I didn't realize that. I just thought it was pretty. What a sweet thing to say. Listen, can you hold on a minute? I'm on the other line. Thanks.

"Andi? It's Adam Tuck. He wanted to tell me how

much he liked my new sweater. He said did I know it brings out the green in my eyes? Gosh, no, Adam, I'd never notice something like that. I just buy the first thing I see. Yes, I know that's not really why he called. Of *course* he wants to ask me to the dance. But the thing is, I'm holding out for— Yeah, okay, go to the bathroom. I'll talk to Adam meanwhile. No, I won't hang up.

"Adam, I'm back. But I've only got a minute because I'm on the other line, so I have to . . . Valentine's Day? Well, I haven't exactly decided yet. I know it's only a week away, but . . . You do? You've already bought the tickets? I know, but the thing is, I sort of made a personal vow that I wouldn't accept any invitations until— Uh, Adam, can I call you back? I have to get back to my other line. Yes, the minute I get off. I promise.

"Andi? I don't know *what* to do. I was just about to tell Adam that I'd made a vow not to go to any dances until the problem of world hunger was solved. Yeah, that could definitely backfire. Yeah, a major crimp in my social life.

"Yes, I know he's farther up the food chain than Mark, but really, don't you think I should be going to a major dance with someone a little cooler than Adam Tuck?

"Oh, stop. I haven't a snobbish bone in my body. I'm just being realistic. I mean, people expect me to have certain *standards*. I don't want to compromise my standards by— I've got another call. Hang on, will you?

"Hi, it's Di. Speak to me.

"Oh, Mark. No, I'm still on the other line. I *said* I'd call you back. Oh, that's sweet, but don't be so impatient. Yes, I promise.

"Andi? I know, I'm sorry. But I don't want to take a chance of missing a call from— *Good grief!* I ought to just turn on the answering machine and let them fight it out among themselves. No, don't hang up. I'll be *one second*, honestly.

"Hello? What? Sure, I'd love a Platinum Card. Absolutely. A ten-thousand-dollar line of credit sounds perfect. Send it right out. What bank account? Only my college fund, which I can't touch, but— Hello? *Hello?* Rats.

"Hey, Andi, I nearly got ten thousand— Oh, darn! Don't answer it. Well, it stops after two boops. See, the thing I wanted to tell you was that I don't want to say yes to anyone until I know for sure whether— Oh, this is ridiculous. No, I have to answer because it might be *him.* No, it's not that my calls are more important than your— Andi, I have to— Andi? Rats.

"Hello? *Derek.* How *are* you? Oh, I'm *so* relieved. I nearly *fainted* when I saw you slam into the backboard last night. I thought, what if Derek is injured so badly he can't *dance*? It would be awful if you had to miss the Sweetheart Stomp.

"Actually, no, I haven't. Well, sure, people have asked me, but . . . no. No, I haven't made any definite plans. Have you? No? That's why you're calling? Oh, Derek, I'm so glad I didn't accept another— What? *Andi?* Yes, I know she's been on the phone for an hour. With me. Then why call *me*? Angry? What makes you think I'm angry? Yes, that's her number. I'm sure I don't know. Ask her yourself. Yeah. So long. Have a nice life."

"Hello, Jason? It's Di. Listen, if you still— Okay, call me back.

"Warren? Hi, this is Di. I know I should have gotten back to you sooner about— Oh. Sure. Talk to you later.

"Hi, Adam. It's me, finally. I know, I know. It's been like Grand Central Station here. Listen, it was awfully sweet of you to ask me to the dance, and I've been thinking over my vow, and— Well, just don't answer it. No, you don't have to. It stops after two—

"Adam? *Adam!* Don't you *dare* put me on hol—!"

Cross Out Where Not Applicable

Dear B.J.,

For a long time I have wanted to tell you I ~~love~~ like you. But every time I try to talk to you I get tongue-tied. So I decided to write this letter instead. I hope I don't get pen-tied! Ha ha.

Ever since the Christmas vacation, when I ran into you, literally, (ha ha!) at the mall I ~~tried to~~ wanted to ~~ask you out~~ ~~tell you how I feel~~ get to know you better.

I would have said something then, when you helped me up, and we were picking up all the presents I dropped. But I felt like ~~such a spaz~~ ~~so clumsy~~ you were in such a hurry that you didn't have time to talk to me.

And I was really ~~embarrassed~~ ~~self-conscious~~ worried about the nightgown. I thought you'd think ~~I was weird~~ I bought it for ~~mysel~~ some girl. I wanted to explain that I wasn't

103

buying it for a girl, I was buying it for my sister. (She's a girl, of course—ha ha!—but I mean, a girlfriend,) ~~which I don't have but the only girl I want is you~~ but I wasn't, I was just buying it because my mother asked me to pick it up for Gina while I was doing my Christmas shopping.

You see how long it would have taken to explain it? Anyway, there were lots of other times after that when I wanted to say something to you. But I could never ~~work up the nerve~~ catch you alone. I usually saw you with your girl friends. A few times you were alone but then I felt like you ~~didn't even notice me~~ ~~didn't know I was alive~~ ~~looked right through me~~ were lost in thought and didn't want to talk to anyone. ~~let alone me~~

Anyway, I think about you ~~so much it's driving me crazy~~ ~~all the time~~ a lot and I finally decided that maybe you were ~~shy too~~ ~~as nervous as me~~ waiting for me to make the first move.

So here it is. My first move. Ha ha. I don't know how you feel about me, or even if you feel <u>anything</u> about me but ~~I'm not sleeping~~

~~nights~~ because of how I feel about you I have
to at least try, so I don't ~~spend the rest of~~
~~my life wondering~~ ~~spend any more sleepless~~
~~nights~~ miss the chance that you might ~~love~~
like me too.

B.J., I think you are really ~~nice~~ ~~cool~~ wonderful and I know it's late to ask, and you
probably already have a date for it, but if
you don't would you go to the Sweetheart
Stomp with me?

I'm ~~a lousy dancer~~ ~~not a very good dancer~~
no Fred Astaire, but I can do slow dances.
~~and those are the dances I'd really like to do~~
~~with you anyway.~~

I want to buy you flowers, and see you in
a fancy dress, and ~~feel my arms around you~~
~~make a really special night of it~~ the whole
nine yards.

I know you're going to think this is sudden, and I should have asked you out to a
movie or something before inviting you to the
dance, because we hardly know each other,
but it's not sudden for me.

I'm going to mail this letter tonight. ~~before~~
~~I chicken out.~~ Please excuse how sloppy it is,

and all the cross-outs. If I take time to recopy it I might ~~lose my nerve~~ not get it to the post office before it closes.

Please don't think I'm a ~~dork~~ ~~a wimp~~ crazy for writing this. ~~I'm only crazy for you.~~

~~Love,~~

~~Sincerely yours,~~

~~Your friend,~~

Love,

Doug (Meyers)

Lucky Break

"Ow!"

"Laurel? What's wrong?" Her mother came to the head of the basement stairs.

"Ow, ow, ow!" Laurel Baker howled. She hopped around the basement, holding her right foot up till she collapsed in a heap next to the weight bench.

Her mother flew down the stairs, Laurel's brother, Benny, right behind her. "What happened?" Benny asked. "Did you hurt yourself?"

"No," Laurel moaned. "I'm screaming for joy."

"What did you do," Benny asked, "drop a dumbbell on your foot?"

"No, I didn't drop a dumbbell on my foot!" Laurel snapped. "I wasn't even working out. Ow. I think my ankle is broken."

"Let me see it." Her mother tried to lift Laurel's foot to examine the injury.

"Ahhhggg!" Laurel screamed. "Don't touch it!"

"It's starting to swell," her mother said.

"Aw, no," Laurel cried. "Not today! I can't break my foot *today.*"

"Benny, help her upstairs," Laurel's mother said. "We'll go to the emergency room."

"I don't want to go to the emergency room!" Laurel wailed. "They'll put me in a cast. I can't dance in a cast."

"You're not going to be able to dance at all," her mother said. "Even if it isn't a break."

"I knew this would happen," Benny said. "I warned you weight lifting was dangerous."

"I tripped!" Laurel cried. "I wasn't even lifting—I was just warming up. And I've been working out for six months, and nothing like this ever—"

"That's enough!" their mother said. "Benny, get her to the car. I'll get an ice pack. Maybe we can keep the swelling down."

"But the dance!" Laurel said. "The Valentine's dance!"

"There'll be other dances," her mother said firmly. "But you have a limited number of feet."

Laurel sat in the backseat of the car, holding a carton of frozen peas against her ankle. "As good as an ice pack," her mother assured her.

"But a lot stupider-looking," Laurel muttered.

Why in the *world* had she worked out today? She should have been lounging in a bubble bath, doing her nails, putting up her hair, setting out her makeup.

That's what normal girls all over Cutter's Forge were doing this Saturday afternoon. And that's what Laurel had planned to do—as soon as she finished her workout.

But her exercise schedule was Tuesday, Thursday, and Saturday, and it had become so much a part of her life that she just didn't feel right when she missed a day. She'd been pumping iron since her fifteenth birthday, and nothing like this had ever happened before.

It wasn't even *her* iron. Benny had gotten the set of weights two Christmases ago. But he'd lost interest in bodybuilding by Easter, and the weights had lain forgotten in a corner of the basement for a year.

Though he'd lost interest in building up his own body, Benny enjoyed watching other people lift weights—mainly, women in skimpy bikinis. One of the cable sports channels showed women's strength competitions almost every week, and Benny talked knowledgeably about abs and quads and something called "definition."

He didn't fool Laurel. She knew he wasn't interested

in abs and quads and definition. He was interested in skimpy bikinis.

The competitors posed and flexed, sometimes doing routines to rock music. They looked so weird! Like they could crack coconuts in their armpits or heft Volvos. Their muscles rippled and bulged. Their arms and legs and thighs ("quads," Benny informed her) were lean and sinewy, with cords of tendons strung taut beneath the skin.

"That's definition," Benny explained.

"That's gross," Laurel said.

But on her fifteenth birthday Laurel took a look at herself in her mirror and didn't like what she saw. This wasn't particularly unusual. Laurel looked in the mirror a lot, and often found something wrong with herself. Her pores were too big. Her chest was too small. Her thighs were too thick. Her lips were too thin.

But that night, dressed to go out for her birthday dinner, Laurel thought she looked like a child's stick figure drawing. Her limbs were positively scrawny. It could have been the black unitard, or the chunky black shoes—but below her knees her legs looked like matchsticks.

Her arms were just as bad. The unitard had short, snug sleeves. They were not flattering. She turned around and peered over her shoulder to see how she looked from behind. Sadly, the back of her looked very much like the front of her. She was round where she wanted to be flat, and flat where she wanted to be round.

She looked like Minnie Mouse.

The next day Laurel carried a load of laundry down to the basement. She dumped it into the washer. Then she headed for the corner where Benny's weights had gathered dust for over a year. She picked up the faintly mildewed instruction booklet that Benny had probably never read: "Getting Acquainted with Your Muscle-master Free Weights."

By the time the washer had finished the spin cycle, Laurel was doing dumbbell curls, front lateral raises, and squats. She knew where her triceps, biceps, and deltoids were. She knew how to increase and decrease weights on the barbells.

The Musclemaster training booklet promised that you could get strong without getting weird-looking. It also promised that you could, in time, transform yourself into an incredible hulk.

She didn't want to be a hulk. She didn't want to look like the women Benny enjoyed watching. She just didn't want to look like Minnie Mouse.

Six months after her first encounter with Benny's

weights, Laurel could look in the mirror and see definition: well-defined arms and calves, firmer thighs, flat-
ter abs. Maybe her new, improved body was the result
of natural growth and development, but by this time
Laurel had come to enjoy her workouts so much that
she'd almost forgotten why she'd started pumping iron
in the first place.

And she'd never had an accident! Never even a
pulled muscle. Her parents worried, and Benny made fun
of her training (probably, she told herself, because she
was now stronger than he was, even though he was two
years older). But she'd never injured herself until today.

Valentine's Day. Six hours before the dance.
How could she have been so *stupid*? It wasn't even an
exercise-related injury. She'd just slipped while warming up, grabbed for the bench to break her fall, and
slammed her foot against the set of barbells.

Mrs. Baker brought the car to a screeching halt in
front of the EMERGENCY ENTRANCE sign on the west side
of the hospital building.

"Get Laurel inside, Benny. I'll park the car."

Benny opened the backdoor and helped Laurel
slide out.

"The ice pack," her mother said. "Take it with you."

"Mom, please!" Laurel begged. "It's not an ice pack. It's frozen peas! I'll look ridiculous."

"They're doctors," Mrs. Baker said. "They've seen worse. Take the peas. You don't know how long you'll have to wait."

Laurel sighed, clutched the package of peas, and hobbled into the emergency room, leaning on Benny's arm.

Most of the plastic chairs inside were occupied by people in various stages of distress. Some were holding red-stained cloths against bleeding wounds. Others were coughing and wheezing. Two children were crying, and one woman with a green-tinged face looked as if she might throw up.

"We'll be here for *hours*," Laurel moaned.

"What difference does it make?" Benny asked. "With that foot there's nothing else you can do except sit."

"But look at all these sick people," Laurel whispered. "I'll probably catch something and be in worse shape than I am now."

"Sit near someone who doesn't look contagious," Benny suggested helpfully.

He led her to a chair next to a man in a postal service uniform. One of the man's ankles was wrapped in a striped dish towel.

"Dog bite?" Benny asked as he sat Laurel down.

"Gunshot," the mailman said.

Laurel grabbed Benny's wrist and dug her finger-nails in. "Crazed postal worker!" she hissed. "Get me away from here!"

"I'm not a crazed postal worker," the mailman assured her. "I just had a little accident. It's only a flesh wound."

Laurel's mother came into the emergency room. She went to the admitting window and handed the nurse her insurance card. She said something to the nurse, who shrugged and handed her a form to fill out.

"That's a good idea, the peas," the mailman said suddenly.

"What?" Laurel eyed him nervously.

"For an ice pack," he explained. "I'd never have thought of that."

"How long have you been waiting?" Benny asked him.

"About an hour."

"For a *gunshot*?" Laurel said.

"It's only a flesh wound," the mailman repeated.

"We'll never get out of here." She sighed.

"What happened to you?" the mailman asked.

"I tripped over a barbell."

The mailman nodded sympathetically. "It's always some silly little thing like that, isn't it?"

Laurel was about to ask him what silly little thing he had done to shoot himself in the foot, but just then her mother sat down next to Benny. She leaned over. "How is it feeling?"

"Cold," Laurel said.

"Does it still hurt as much?"

"It's numbing up," Laurel said.

Mrs. Baker looked at the ankle. "It's still swollen," she said. "But it could be just a sprain."

"Well, whatever it is," Laurel said, "I don't think I'm going to be dancing on it tonight."

"I know." Her mother patted her arm. "I'm sorry. You were looking forward to the dance so much."

"Yeah."

She had been looking forward to the Sweetheart Stomp, even though she hadn't expected a particularly romantic evening.

She and Teddy were not sweethearts, just friends. But since neither of them had a sweetheart, they'd decided they might as well go to the dance together.

They'd each paid for their own tickets and agreed to split all expenses. They planned on doubling with Teddy's student exchange houseguest, Alexei, and

Jamie (who now called herself Janushka) Farrentino.

Even if she hadn't expected romance, Laurel had expected fun. She'd bought a slinky eggshell silk dress with a broad gold belt, which made her new, improved body look even more improved.

"I have to call Teddy!" she said suddenly. She started to get up and fell back into the seat. "I can't stand up."

"Benny can call him for you," her mother said.

"What should I tell him?" Benny asked.

Laurel snapped, "Tell him I've become a nun! What do you *think* you should tell him?"

The mailman leaned over and tapped her on the shoulder. "My sister's a nun," he said. "It's a very secure job. Like the postal service."

Laurel squirmed in her seat and tried to signal her mother that she wanted to get away from this nut.

"Kerwin Slaney!" the nurse called.

"That's me." The mailman stood up and gingerly put his injured foot on the floor. He winced. "Good luck," he said to Laurel.

"You too." Laurel was relieved as he limped toward the admitting window.

Mrs. Baker reached into her pocketbook. "And get us something to read, Benny," she said. "We could be here awhile."

"We could be here *forever*," Laurel said. "This might be hell, and for all eternity, we'll—"

"No," her mother said firmly. "Hell is when your child is in pain and there isn't any hospital."

"Oh, for Pete's sake," Laurel grumbled. "You don't have to be so . . . so . . . *motherly*."

"I'm sorry, dear." She patted Laurel's hand. "I'll try to be more cold and unfeeling."

In spite of herself Laurel smiled. She squeezed her mother's hand. "Sorry, I'm sulking," she said. "But I can't help it. This is just such rotten timing."

"It is," Mrs. Baker agreed. "Though there's probably never a good time to fall over a barbell."

"Maybe the day before a math test," Laurel said.

Benny eventually returned to the waiting room. "I called Ted." He sat down in the chair Kerwin Slaney had vacated. "He said to tell you that his heart was broken."

"Did he really say that?" Laurel asked, startled.

"No. But I thought it would make you feel better."

"Gee, thanks," Laurel said sarcastically. "What did he really say?"

"He said he was sorry you couldn't make the dance, he hoped it wasn't anything serious, and Happy Valentine's Day."

He dropped a magazine into her lap and passed a newspaper across her to their mother.

"Why did you get me this?" Laurel cried. "Are you trying to be funny?" It was a magazine called *Iron Maidens*. On the cover was a picture of a muscular blond woman in biker shorts and a tank top, flexing one arm to display a biceps the size of a grapefruit.

"It's about women's weight training," Benny said. "I thought you'd be interested."

"Well, I'm not," Laurel snapped.

Benny took the magazine from her. "Okay, I'll read it."

"Laurel Baker!" the admitting nurse called.

Laurel dropped the frozen peas into Benny's lap and stood up, putting her weight on her uninjured foot. Her mother helped her to the window.

"She can go on up to X-ray now," the nurse said. "You can wait here for her."

"But she can't walk."

"She doesn't have to," the nurse said. "Mason will take her."

"Who's—" Laurel stopped before she could finish the question. A young man pushing a wheelchair appeared, as if by magic, from around the corner.

"Hi," he said. "Want a ride?"

Laurel stared at his (extremely) blue eyes, his appealingly shaggy hair, his reassuring smile. She eased herself into the wheelchair.

"Will you be okay by yourself?" her mother asked.

"She'll be fine," Mason promised. "I'll take good care of her."

Laurel's heart fluttered, momentarily making her forget about her throbbing ankle. "I'll be okay," she told her mother. "I guess someone'll tell you if they have to do anything major."

"Definitely," Mason said. "They won't do any procedure without getting your permission first."

"All right then." Mrs. Baker bent down and gave her a gentle hug. "Good luck."

Mason wheeled her around the corner and down a long corridor. "X-ray's on the fourth floor," he said. "Just a short trip on the elevator."

"I already had a short trip today."

"How did it happen?" Mason asked.

"Oh, it's too dumb to tell," she said. "You're not a doctor, are you?"

"No, I'm just a candy striper."

Laurel twisted her head around to look at him. "You're not wearing stripes." He had on a blue cotton jacket that matched his eyes. An embroidered patch over one pocket read HUNTERDON HOSPITAL, VOLUNTEER.

"Hardly anybody does anymore," he said. "I just get a kick out of saying I'm a candy striper. It shakes up people's expectations. Everyone thinks only girls volunteer at hospitals."

He stopped the wheelchair at the bank of elevators at the end of the corridor. He pushed a button. Laurel hoped the elevator would take a long time to reach them.

"You like to do that?" Laurel asked.

"What? Surprise people, or work at the hospital?"

The elevator doors opened. *Rats,* Laurel thought. Mason waited until everyone in the car got out, then wheeled her inside and pressed a button. He turned her so she faced the door, and stood beside her so she could see him.

"I meant surprise people," Laurel said. "But do you like working here?"

"Of course," he said. "Otherwise I wouldn't do it."

"What kinds of things do you do?" she asked. "Besides giving people rides?"

The elevator suddenly shuddered and stopped. Were they on the fourth floor already? Laurel looked up at the row of numbers over the door. None of them was lit.

"Oh, not again!" Mason pressed a button, waited a

moment, then pressed another button. Nothing happened.

"What's wrong?" Laurel asked.

"I knew we should have waited for the other elevator," Mason said.

"Why? What happened?"

"Now, don't panic," Mason said. "It's just a little temperamental, that's all. Sometimes, if you press the right series of buttons, it starts up again."

He pushed some more buttons. The elevator didn't move.

"This stupid elevator has had problems since I've been here," Mason said.

"Problems?" Laurel asked nervously. "Like cables snapping and people plunging down—"

"No, no, nothing like that," Mason said. "It just gets stuck. I'll push the alarm. Don't get scared at the noise."

"I thought you weren't supposed to make noise in a hospital," Laurel said.

"You can when it's an emergency." Mason pushed a red button, and Laurel shrieked as a clanging bell went off.

"It's okay, it's okay." Mason put his hands on her shoulders and bent down so she was looking directly into his (deep, sincere) eyes.

Laurel clutched at his hand and held it until the clanging stopped.

"Don't worry," he said calmly. "We'll be out of here in no time."

"How long is 'no time'?"

"Well . . ." He hesitated. "On a weekday, it'd be only a few minutes. It's a little trickier digging up an engineer on a weekend."

"How long?" Laurel repeated.

"Oh, an hour. Two, tops. Depends." Mason leaned against the elevator railing and folded his arms across his chest.

"Two hours?" She wasn't sure if she was pleased that she would be alone with Mason for two hours, or scared about being trapped in a small, enclosed cell.

"That's the worst-case scenario," he said. "It almost never takes that long."

Laurel took a few deep breaths. "And you're sure the cable won't break?"

"Positive. The worst that can happen is that you'll get bored."

"What about air?" she asked. "Will we have enough air?"

"Hey, you're in a hospital. There's oxygen all over the place."

Laurel smiled. He was one of the handsomest boys she'd ever seen. And sweet, too. Concerned about her, sensitive to her feelings, anxious to keep her from being upset.

There were worse things than being trapped in an elevator with him, she thought. For instance, she could be trapped in an elevator with Benny.

"What do you do here besides wheeling people around?" she asked again.

"Oh, lots of things. Deliver meals, feed people, run errands, bring around the library cart. Sometimes I do my puppet act in the children's ward."

"You do a puppet act?" Laurel asked. "That's neat."

"Actually, it's pretty stupid." Mason grinned. "But if you're young enough and sick enough, I guess it's not bad."

"Do your act for me," Laurel said.

"I can't." He looked embarrassed. "I don't have Pinky with me."

"Pinky?" Laurel grinned.

"I told you it was dumb."

"Hey in there!" a distant voice called. "You okay?"

"No one's dying!" Mason shouted back. "But I've got a kid with a real bad foot."

Kid? Laurel thought.

Mason must have read her mind. "They work faster if they think it's a kid," he said.

"There's a short somewhere," the voice called. "We'll find it."

Mason squatted down next to Laurel's chair. "See? Everything'll be okay. Why don't you tell me about yourself. Like, how did you injure your foot?"

Laurel hesitated a moment; then she thought, *Oh, why not? He probably does think I'm just a kid. He must see hundreds of patients like me. Besides, complaining will help pass the time.*

So she told him. About the weight training, about falling against the barbell, about the Sweetheart Stomp. Even about her slinky new dress.

"That's a shame," he said when she finally finished. "You really like this Teddy, huh?"

"We're just friends," Laurel said. "But the dance would have been fun. You don't go to Cutter's Forge High, do you?"

"No, Hunterdon. We're having a Valentine's dance tonight too."

"That's nice." Laurel sighed. "Are you going with your girlfriend?"

"I don't have a girlfriend," he said. "And I'm working here till nine."

Laurel couldn't believe it. How could someone like Mason not have girls hurling themselves at him? *Maybe,* she thought, *he means he doesn't have a* steady *girlfriend. Maybe he goes out with a different girl every week.*

"We'll probably be in this elevator till nine," Laurel said.

Mason smiled. "Would that be so bad?" he asked.

Laurel gulped. "Well, we might get hungry," she said weakly. Was he suggesting that he didn't mind being alone in the elevator with her? That he actually *liked* it? That he might even like *her*?

"I'm not hungry," Mason said. "Are you?"

Laurel was about to respond when the elevator gave a jerk and a groan. She gasped, and Mason grabbed the handle of her wheelchair.

"It's all right," he said. "They've got it fixed. How does the ankle feel?"

"I forgot all about it," Laurel said truthfully.

"Must be my sparkling conversation," Mason said.

They reached the fourth floor. Laurel held her breath and waited for the door to open. When it did, she was relieved. But her feelings were definitely mixed. Mason would deliver her to the X-ray lab and go off to take care of another patient. She would never see him again.

Sure, she felt safer out of the elevator than trapped in it. But she was already beginning to miss Mason.

He wheeled her down the hall. She wanted to turn and see his face again but didn't. What was the point? They had had a chance meeting in a hospital, where he met hundreds of people every week. He would forget about her by the time he got back to the emergency room.

"This is the worst Valentine's Day of my whole life," she said softly.

"You keep track of them?" he asked.

"Not usually," she said. "It's just that this one's outstanding in its awfulness."

"Here we are." Mason wheeled her into a small waiting area next to a door marked X-RAY LAB. There were two other people ahead of her.

"Thank you." Laurel had never believed in love at first sight. She'd never even thought about love at first sight, unless she was watching a movie or reading a romance novel. But Mason was cute and sweet and special. He cared about people, did puppet shows for sick kids. Maybe what she was feeling wasn't exactly love, but it was certainly intense like.

"Don't be so down," he said gently. "There'll be other dances."

"That's what my mother says. But my beautiful dress . . ." She knew how stupid that sounded. Yet she couldn't tell him the rest of the reason for her dejection.

He knelt down next to her. "You know what I think? I think you should wear that dress tonight. Even if you can't go to the dance."

"Why?" Laurel looked up at him, puzzled. "No one will see it."

He pulled a small notepad and a Bic pen from his pocket.

"I will," he said. "If you'll give me your address."

"What?"

"You're not going to your dance," he said. "And I'm not going to my dance. And it's Valentine's Day. Let's celebrate it together."

Laurel couldn't answer. She could hardly breathe.

He put the pen and pad in her lap. "Come on," he said. "If you want, I'll even bring Pinky and do my act for you."

"Really?"

"Sure. But I'm warning you, it's awfully lame. No pun intended."

"I don't care," she said softly. She wrote her name and address on the pad and handed it to Mason.

He looked at the paper, smiled, and tucked the pad back in his pocket.

The PA system beeped. "Volunteer staff! Volunteer staff! Emergency room!"

"That's me," Mason said. "I hate to leave you alone, but I have to go."

"That's okay." Laurel smiled. "I'll see you tonight, I guess."

"I get off at nine. I'll be at your house by nine seventeen." He looked down at her foot. "I hope it's not broken," he added.

If it is, Laurel thought, *it's almost worth it.* Aloud, all she said was "Thanks."

"You know," Mason said, his hand lingering on the back of her wheelchair, "I'm really glad I'm a candy striper."

Laurel smiled shyly. "I'm really glad I'm a weight lifter." She watched Mason jog down the hall. The door of the elevator they'd been stuck in opened. He hesitated, turned, and waved to her.

"Think I'll use the stairs," he called. "I don't want to be late for our dance."

At the Stomp

*J*amie (Janushka) Farrentino rested her cheek against Alexei's shoulder as they swayed to the romantic rhythms of Yellow Fever. Jamie was surprised that Yellow Fever knew any romantic rhythms. Their sound was principally twangs, drums, and amplified screeches, which made dancing difficult and earplugs desirable.

"Is beautiful," Alexei whispered into her ear.

"The music?"

"The decorations," he said. "The gym. Whole thing very festive."

"Yes." Jamie admired the surroundings. Pink and red heart-shaped balloons floated overhead. Cardboard cupids, streamers of *X*s and *O*s and huge paper roses hung everywhere.

"You are fine decoration too," Alexei said. "Prettiest decoration here."

"Oh, Alexei." Jamie looked away, embarrassed, as

his dark eyes searched her face. She fixed her attention on Amy Porter and Batso. Batso was lumbering around the floor like an overweight bear, though he was not fat and certainly not fuzzy. For some reason he was suddenly, shockingly, bald.

The music trailed off listlessly, as if the band had gotten bored with the song.

"You are very good dancer," Alexei said as they separated.

"Not as good as you," Jamie said. "You're the best dancer in school."

"You should see me do lambada," Alexei said.

Jamie giggled. "I don't think they're going to play a lambada," she said. "It's not exactly the latest thing."

"Oh." Alexei looked disappointed. "Is golden oldie?"

"Well, it's an oldie," Jamie said.

"Jamie!" Di Callahan greeted her like a long-lost sister reunited on a talk show. She was grasping Mark Chetwin's wrist, and Jamie got the feeling she'd had to drag him over to where she and Alexei were standing.

"Alexei," Di purred, "I had no idea you were such a wonderful dancer."

"Thank you."

"How about changing partners?" she suggested.

Mark scowled. Jamie scowled. Alexei wrinkled his forehead.

"Into what?" he asked.

Her laugh tinkled prettily, like wind chimes. Jamie wondered how long she'd practiced it.

"I mean, for the next dance. You dance with me, and Jamie dances with Mark."

"When is next dance?" Alexei asked, his face innocent. "Spring Swing?"

"I don't mean the next *school* dance," Di began, "I mean—"

But just then Yellow Fever exploded into another number, and Alexei grabbed Jamie's hand. "Excuse, please!"

He twirled her away to the middle of the floor. Jamie had to bite her lip to keep from laughing. Lucky for her, Alexei's English was still limited.

"You don't mind?" Alexei shouted over the music. "You did not want to dance with Mark?"

"You mean you *did* understand her?" Jamie shouted back.

"Of course," Alexei said. "What do you think, I am born today?"

B.J. Green and Doug Meyers stood next to the punch bowl. The dance was their first date. They were still shy with each other, so they covered their nervousness by drinking a lot of punch.

Doug had told the truth in his letter. He was no Fred Astaire. But B.J. didn't mind. She was no Ginger Rogers. And the night was romantic, and she was with a boy who'd admired her from afar for months.

She was pretty sure she'd never been admired from afar before, and she was positive she'd never been admired up close. It was so amazing, so mystical. She'd never gotten to make a third wish at Antonelli's fountain, yet one had come true anyway.

Doug took a big gulp of punch and moved closer to her. "This is the first dance I ever went to," he confessed. "I hope I'm doing everything right."

"You must be," B.J. said, surprised that the words came to her so easily. "Because I'm having a wonderful time."

Andi and Derek staggered toward them, looking exhausted. "Water!" Andi gasped. *"Water!"*

Derek groaned, and then he dipped out two cups of punch. He handed one to Andi and chugalugged his. Andi wiped her forehead and panted.

"What's wrong?" B.J. asked.

"This music's too fast for me." Derek gripped the edge of the table for support.

"You're a *basketball* player," Doug said. "How can the music be too fast for you?"

"This isn't basketball." Derek swigged down another cup of punch. "Whole different set of muscles."

"Are you having a good time, B.J.?" Andi asked, between wheezes.

"Super," B.J. said. "Your committee did a great job."

"Thank you. I think— Will you look at *that!*" Andi leaned against the table and stared out at the dance floor. "I don't believe it!"

B.J. looked. There, in the middle of the gym, was Robert La Motte. His arms were draped around Mimi Ostermeyer, and her arms were draped around him. Their feet were moving, sort of, to some beat that no one else heard. Their steps certainly had no relationship to the frantic music Yellow Fever was performing.

B.J. and Andi weren't the only ones staring. Half the dancers on the floor were maneuvering to get a glimpse of Robert La Motte with an actual girl on an actual date.

"At least he's not trying to do a tango," B.J. said, remembering her nightmare wish.

"A tango!" Andi nearly dropped her punch. "It's a miracle he can move sideways and hold Mimi at the same time."

Yellow Fever finally took a break. The area around the refreshment table got crowded, and B.J. and Doug drifted away from the feeding frenzy.

Jamie—Janushka, B.J. reminded herself—limped toward them, led by Alexei, who didn't look the least bit winded.

"Swell dance!" he said. He peered over the crowd at the table. "Looks like swell refreshments, too."

"You must have dances in Russia," Doug said.

"Oh, yes, of course," Alexei said. "But not such swell refreshments. And not Janushka."

B.J. couldn't tell if Jamie was blushing or just flushed from the exertion of the last dance. But for an exhausted person she sure looked happy.

Alexei went to get them some food.

"Weren't you supposed to come with Teddy and Laurel?" Doug asked. "I haven't seen them yet."

"They're not here," Jamie said. "Laurel banged up her ankle. She was at Hunterdon Hospital all afternoon."

"That's terrible!" B.J. said. "Is it broken?"

"Well, it's not broken. But she can't walk on it."

"What lousy luck," Doug sympathized.

"Not as lousy as you might think," Jamie said knowingly.

"Huh?"

"It's a long story." Jamie grinned. "But as a matter of fact, it's *perfect* for Valentine's Day. . . ."

CRUSH

√ **DATE DUE** 24396
